Rockett's World

CAN YOU KEEP A SECRET?

Read more about

Rockett's World

in:

#1 WHO CAN YOU
TRUST?
#2 WHAT KIND OF
FRIEND ARE YOU?
#3 ARE WE THERE
YET?
#5 WHERE DO YOU
BELONG?

Purple Moon

Rockett's World

CAN YOU KEEP A SECRET?

Lauren Day

SCHOLASTIC INC.

New York Toronto London Auckland Sydney
Mexico City New Delhi Hong Kong

ISBN 0-439-08210-2

12 11 10 9 8 7 6 5 4 3 2 1   0 1 2 3 4 5/0

Printed in the U.S.A.   40
First Scholastic printing, January 2000

Rockett's World

CAN YOU KEEP A SECRET?

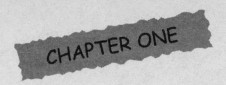

CHAPTER ONE

"Rockett! I have to tell you something. It's about Miko. Has girlfriend been acting weird lately, or is it just me picking up these vibes?"

Rockett scrunched her forehead and read the e-mail from her friend Nakili. The girls were sitting a few partitioned cubes away from each other in computer science lab. The class was supposed to be creating study grids on their screens, not passing instant messages.

Of course, that's what most people were doing anyway. But with e-mail at everyone's fingertips, it was like being given pen and paper — and then told, "Don't use it for notes."

Except Nakili Abuto, one of Rockett's closest buds at Whistling Pines Junior High, usually didn't. Nakili, as bubbly and social as anyone, usually wasn't a huge note passer or whisperer. *She must really be wiggin' about Miko, one of her best friends*, Rockett thought.

Rockett shifted in her seat, and began to write back. She'd gotten as far as "I know! Miko's been . . ." when she got another message: Unsurprisingly, Dana St. Clair was on-line, sticking her cyber nose in, copying both Nakili and Rockett.

She'd written, "I wanted to talk to *you*, N, about that — Miko's been all gloomy-girl lately."

To which Nakili quipped, "It's almost like she's morphed into you, Dana!"

Rockett reacted with a giggle, and quickly typed, "At least Miko's not being snarky. Which means the Dana-to-Miko personality transplant isn't complete: We can still hope."

There! I gave it right back — or did Dana think I missed her pointed little "I wanted to talk to you, N . . ." If that girl ever gets over trying to make me feel so not a part of their group, I'll know world peace has finally been achieved.

Dana, sitting on the opposite side of the classroom, stood up to give Rockett a real — as opposed to virtual — sneer. Just before Ms. Chen, their teacher, ordered her to sit down, she quickly wrote, "If I'm snarky, it's only to certain deserving individuals."

Rockett could practically hear Nakili grumbling as she typed — in all capitals, so Rocket and Dana would understand she was yelling — "ENOUGH, YOU TWO! You have now entered a no-cyber-sniping zone. Let's get back to Miko. The girl is just not right, and as her friends, you both should want to find out what's up. Friends don't let friends take up permanent residence on planet Glum. Got that?"

Chastised, both Dana and Rockett wrote back, agreeing.

Rockett noted, "Here's what really surprised me. Instead of working with us and Mr. Rarebit on the extra-credit art assignment after school, she hung out to watch boys' soccer team practice instead! I don't get it."

Across the room, Rockett could see Nakili vigorously nodding in agreement as she typed, "Yeah, wussup with that? Usually girlfriend is all about art. . . ."

". . . and Mr. Rarebit!" Dana had to stick that in. Everyone knew Miko kind of had a crush on their art teacher.

Nakili thought of something else. "And instead of having lunch with us yesterday, she spent the period in the library. Only kids needing extra help are there that period — which she doesn't!"

Rockett tilted her head and mused, "Possible she's tutoring someone?"

Dana dashed off, "Don't you think we'd know that?"

Like they'd know and I wouldn't? Don't think I didn't catch that! Rockett was about to spout a clever comeback, but what popped onto her screen — written by Nakili — stopped her. "Here's the worst of it. In language arts class, when Mrs. Tinydahl called on Cleve to recite the last line of the 'To be or not to be' soliloquy and he gave that stupid answer? So Mrs. T goes, 'At least we can count on one student to know the correct answer. Miko? For Mr. Goodstaff's edification, would you please recite the soliloquy as Mr. Shakespeare intended it?' And Miko spaces! She goes, 'I . . . uh . . . what was that again?' Instead of doing the stand-and-deliver thing, she shrunk back in her seat! Wussup with that?"

Dana typed, "Sounds like a split personality: more Meek-o than Miko!"

"Can't be a self-esteem meltdown," Nakili decided. "Girlfriend just won the haiku-writing contest."

"And she blew away the competition in the chess tournament, too," Dana reminded them.

Then Rockett thought of something. "Dumb question alert. Did either of you just ask her what's wrong?"

Typing in tandem — using almost the same words — her friends replied, "Well, duh. But she blows us off!"

"It's like she just doesn't trust us or something," Dana added.

"Maybe she doesn't even know what's wrong," Rockett ventured, "or . . . growing pains or something . . ."

"Ms. Rockett Movado! Unless you're creating a growing pains grid, I don't see how what's on your screen has anything to do with our lesson. Would you care to enlighten us?"

Because Rockett had totally not heard Ms. Chen sneak up behind her, she practically jumped out of her seat at the teacher's reprimand. She went into automatic spin control. But even as the words tumbled out, she knew how lame they sounded. "I'm . . . uh . . . I was almost done with it. And . . ."

Rrrriiiiinngg! Usually Rockett rolled her eyes at clichés, but the one Ms. Chen used just then sounded totally sweet: "Saved by the bell!"

Quickly, Rockett shut down her computer. Her screen went dark.

4

Ms. Chen shook her head. "This is unlike you, Rockett. But I expect you will hand in your study grid, perfectly, tomorrow."

Lunch period was next, so Rockett, Nakili, and Dana headed to their lockers for a pit stop. Nakili noted, "Come to think of it, there's so much Miko doesn't want to talk about lately. She wouldn't even show me her winning poem."

Rockett bit her lip. *Maybe she doesn't want to be friends with them anymore and doesn't know how to say it. That can't be . . . can it? Well, no way I can broach that one!*

As if reading her mind, Nakili mused, "Maybe Miko is feeling, you know, that things aren't how they used to be on the friendship train. Don't get me wrong, but, Dana . . . you have been spending more time with Ginger lately."

"Ginger rocks!" Dana shot back, instantly defensive. Then she pointed out, "Of course, you've been hanging with Rockett."

Nakili scoffed, "So? Chilling with other people doesn't mean we're not friends with her. Miko knows that!"

"Something else," Dana mentioned. "That outfit she wore yesterday? All in black. And those platforms? They must have been her sister's, because that is so not her. She was walking down the hallway with Cleve — and let's take a moment to barf at that one" — Dana mimed sticking her finger down her throat — "and she was almost as tall as him!"

5

"That's *it*!" Rockett felt like she'd been hit by a lightning bolt. Without thinking, she whirled around and blurted out, "It's Cleve!"

Dana asked, "What's Cleve?"

"Don't you see it?" Rockett exclaimed. "Cleve's the link."

"Cleve's a fink?" Dana drawled, delighted with herself. "How new."

"Could you just *listen* for a minute and mute the clever? All the strange things Miko's been doing lately — Cleve's *been* there. Boys' soccer, the library during tutoring period — I heard his grades *are* slipping. Pretending she didn't know the soliloquy in language arts, didn't that come right after Cleve's goof? And walking down the hall with him. You just said it yourself. She's . . . hanging with . . . uh . . . Cleve. . . ." Rockett trailed off. Because even as she put all the pieces together, the scenario did sound beyond ridiculous.

Ditto to Nakili.

"That's whack! You're sayin' Miko's moving away from us . . . toward Cleve Goodstaff and his crowd?"

In a faux deep voice, Dana leaned in and whispered, "She's gone to the dark side."

Everyone knew Cleve was all about popularity — in the most superficial way. Tall, blond, athletic, and flirty, Cleve was a total FON: Friend of Nicole. That is, Nicole "The One" Whittaker, founder and moving force behind the school's snobbiest clique. A bunch of kids who, apart from the pack, could actually be nice — but when together acted like they had a lock on coolness.

Something Rockett, Nakili, and Dana totally didn't buy into.

That went double for Miko. Usually.

Nakili stopped short and narrowed her eyes. "Cut to the chase, girlfriends. Something's not right with Miko. Reason? Unknown. But here's what we do know. She's pullin' away from us — and when she's around, she's either withdrawn and glum, or a chill-pill, blowing us off, rushing in the other direction. Hypothesis? Maybe we did something that hurt her."

"But what?" Rockett asked.

"Maybe it's what we didn't do," Dana said thoughtfully.

Rockett had no clue what she meant, but Nakili got it instantly. "You mean because we didn't make a big deal when she won those two contests — the chess thing and the poetry thing? I didn't call to congratulate her — did you?"

Dana shrugged. "No, but that's because Miko and major awardage are synonymous. It's not like we have to throw her a party every time she adds another trophy to her collection, but maybe she feels —"

"Snap!" Nakili interrupted. Eyes aglow, she snapped her fingers.

Rockett and Dana stopped in their tracks. "Snap?" Rockett asked.

"We throw her a party!" Nakili exclaimed.

Dana crinkled her forehead. "Huh? Wanna reboot that for me?"

"What *part* of part-y didn't you get?" Nakili challenged, adding, "We'll wrench Miko out of pity city by throwing a full-tilt, all-about-Miko, CSG-sponsored surprise party. All on board, say hey!"

Rockett hesitated. "You think she'd really . . . want that?"

"On the real, she just won all this stuff. Winning's all the sweeter if you have friends to share it with. As her closest friends, we *get* that — okay, so better late than never. It'll bring us all back together. Oh, yeah! This is brilliant!" Nakili was thrilled with herself. Gleefully, she threw open her locker.

"Ouch!" Dana suddenly screamed and grasped her forearm.

"Nakili's party idea wasn't *that* hurtin'," Rockett teased.

"It's not that!" Dana blasted. "Some idiot just hit me with a rubber band." She whirled around. No one was in sight, but the distinct muffled sounds of boy laughter could be heard from around the corner.

"Oops, another attack by the invisible finger," Rockett giggled.

"Ruben did this. I know it," Dana growled. "He did the same thing last week. I'm gonna get him."

"No way!" Rockett reacted without thinking. She was

sorry, too. Because it gave Dana the perfect opportunity to taunt her.

"Oh, defend him, why don't you? Just because he's your little crush-boy, you would!"

"I do not have a crush on him, and you know it, Dana."

"You so do. And the whole school knows it. The question is what you see in him — he's a little brat." Dana rubbed her arm for emphasis.

Nakili slammed her locker shut and got in both their faces. "You!" she commanded Dana. "Lemme look at your arm."

Obediently, Dana held it out.

Nakili shook her head. "No marks. Only your ego got bruised, so deal. And you." She turned to Rockett. "You don't know if Ruben did it or not, so quit defending —"

Rockett held up her hand. "My bad, Nakili. I don't know who did it. But Ruben Rosales is not my cr —"

Nakili frowned. "Lookit, girlfriends, Miko's meeting us in about two minutes in the cafeteria, so we're not gonna have a lot of time, y'know what I'm sayin'?"

Rockett nodded. "A surprise party has to be planned without her knowledge."

"Logistics alert," Dana said. "When would we have it? Where would we have it? Who would we invite?"

"Easy, easier, and easiest," was Nakili's snap response.

"Playing the parts of speech game is always fun," Dana threw back at her, "but get real. Answer the questions."

Rockett piped up, "You probably should do it kinda soon, right? Maybe the weekend after next would be good."

"And we could have it at my house," Nakili added — then did a quick U-ie. "Scratch that. Construction of the new family room. Not gonna happen. How 'bout your place?" She looked at Dana hopefully.

"Doubtful. The evil stepsister factor: Rachel would have to be involved."

Before Rockett could even think about offering, Dana did a verbal delete. "Forget about your house, it's a CSG-run fiesta."

She sets, she shoots, she scores! Another goal for Dana!

Nakili lit up. "What about the rec room at the swim club? Or that huge room in the community center? They rent out for parties."

"Great idea, Nakili, except for two *reea-lly* big problems," Dana detailed, counting off on her fingers: "'muh' and 'knee'! As treasurer of the CSG bank account, I can tell you our reserves are not that high."

Nakili sighed. "I could break into the personal piggy bank, maybe. . . ."

Should I offer to help out? I bet if three of us chipped in, we'd have enough to rent the rec room. But I can barely get a word in before Dana steps all over me. Why give her another chance? I should just let the two of them figure it out and go as a guest. On the other hand, if I did chip in, I could probably be part of the planning. Which would be total fun. I should just say something. But then how lame will I feel if they both turn me down?

10

Confession Session

Could Dana be right? Have we been letting Miko down, not being there for her? It can't be because I've been chillin' with Rockett. Miko likes Rockett. And it doesn't bother me that Dana hangs with Ginger sometimes. But maybe it bothers Miko. Maybe it's true. The sista-hood is kinda goin' through some changes. But the party will fix all that!

I knew this would happen. It has nothing to do with Ginger — I wish her birthday fell in Sagittarius, so I could make her a CSG — but it has everything to do with Rockett. Now Miko's feeling it. As if a party will change anything! No way!

CHAPTER TWO

"I have some money saved up. I could chip in." Purposely, Rockett didn't look at Dana but braced herself for a diss, even as she tried to duck it by adding, "Don't worry, you two would still make all the major decisions. I'm not trying to horn in, but I want to help. If this'll make Miko feel better, I'm all over it."

A megawatt smile illuminated Nakili's face as she threw an arm around Rockett. "Girl, you rock! We're gonna do this — all of us." She elbowed Dana gently, a gesture Rockett probably wasn't supposed to notice, but did.

Dana made a face — this time Rockett was pretty sure it was for her benefit — as she pushed open the doors to the school lunchroom. As usual during fifth period, it was barely controlled chaos, jam-packed with exuberant students letting off major steam. "We're gonna have to table this discussion," Dana remarked, pointing to the regular CSG spot, "since the guest of honor is already at our table."

Miko must have gotten there early. She'd been through the lunch line and was sipping her iced tea and writing in a notebook. If she noticed her friends walking toward her, she didn't show it.

"Sit with us today, Rockett," Nakili urged, shooting Dana a "better not object" look.

I'd like that, but would it seem weird? I always sit with Jessie. Who always sits with Darnetta. And Mavis, she sometimes sits with us, too. Rockett glanced over at her usual table.

Jessie Marbella was the first friend Rockett had made at Whistling Pines. They'd just bonded naturally. After settling in, Rockett had made many more friends — some, like Nakili, had definite best friend potential. One thing about Rockett — she was all over balancing different friendships.

Jessie and Darnetta were side by side, in an animated convo. Then, as Jessie realized Rockett was looking at them, she glanced up, caught Rockett's eye, and waved.

So what if I don't sit with them today? No big, right? Rockett motioned that she was joining the CSG table. Jessie's face clouded for a sec, but then Darnetta said something that made her laugh. In a flash, Jessie shrugged and turned her attention to her friend.

Relieved, Rockett advanced with Nakili and Dana toward their table. Miko nodded but said nothing.

So Rockett greeted her. "Were you first in line or something?"

Glancing up through her trademark black wingtip glasses, Miko shrugged. "Got here a couple of minutes early."

Nakili pointed to her tray and made a face. "What was that in its former life? Some macaroni and some cheese-like substance? What other rank choices do we have today?"

Normally, Miko would have made some joke about the quality-control-challenged choices. The place was run — more like, commandeered — by the aptly named Mr. Pill, who seemed to have a "bad taste" in his mouth for all the kids. Not to mention how bad his food tasted!

But, as her friends had been noticing, Miko had journeyed far, far from the land of normal. In answer to Nakili's question, she gazed away and murmured, "The usual. There might be pizza."

"O-kay." Dana, clearly uneasy about Miko's attitude, dumped her books on the table, with a little more force than necessary. "Think I'll just go see for myself."

Nakili sat down, positioning herself directly opposite Miko. For a split sec, Rockett thought she might confront their suddenly gloomy friend. But Nakili just looked at her and offered, "Hey, girl, if you need someone to talk to . . . I'm always here."

Miko looked genuinely puzzled. But instead of making eye contact with Nakili, she shifted her gaze and scanned the room, remarking, "I don't know what would give you that impression. I'm fine."

Rockett followed Miko's gaze — straight to The Ones' "must-be-seen" table, situated center stage of the lunchroom. Nicole and her posse, Whitney Weiss and Stephanie Hollis, were there. The school's reigning fashionistas, decked out in practically identical twin sets and miniskirts,

14

were digging into little white boxes rimmed with wire handles. A sure sign of takeout.

"I guess a few certain someones in our school have found an alternative to what passes for nutrition here," Rockett remarked.

"Who? What are you talking about?" Miko spun around a little too quickly, as if she'd just been busted.

"Nicole, Whitney, and Stephanie," Rockett said. "You were just looking at them, weren't you?"

"No," Miko denied, "I totally wasn't looking at anyone."

Excuse me! She so was. Of course, that's where Cleve usually sits. Wonder if she was . . . ? No. Can't be.

On awkward-moment patrol, Nakili said, "Don't know about you, Rockett, but that sound I just heard? Rumbling stomach! Gonna come with me to the lunch line?"

"Sure." But just as Rockett and Nakili got up, Dana returned. She had a tray in hand, and a friend by her side.

Ginger Baskin. She usually hung with Arrow Mayfield and Viva Cortez, with whom she was part of a rock band.

"Hey, Ginger," Nakili greeted her warmly, "chillin' with us today?"

Ginger nodded hopefully. "If that's cool . . . ?"

" 'Course it is," Nakili responded. "C'mon, Rockett, let's jet to the line before even the barfaroni is gone."

As Dana slipped onto the bench seat next to Miko, Rockett heard her say — pointedly — "You guys haven't

15

heard Arrow and the Explorers recently. They've gotten so much better. Good enough to start playing at parties, right, Ginger?"

The second they were out of earshot, Rockett said, "Could Dana have been any more obvious? She's already campaigning for Ginger to play at Miko's party."

Nakili grinned and grabbed a tray. "Nothin' wrong with that, is there? Unless, of course, you were gonna suggest another band?"

Rockett practically jumped down Nakili's throat. "I was not! I mean, I wasn't even thinking about anything."

"Down, girl!" Nakili teased. "You're gonna tell me the thought of Ruben and Rebel Angels playing never entered your mind?"

Eyes squarely on the sandwich selection, Rockett flinched. "We just decided to have the party like three minutes ago, so no. I hadn't thought about it. But . . ." Settling on egg salad on a roll, she ventured, "Now that you mention it, Ruben's band is totally tight. And I bet they'd play just for the experience. We wouldn't have to pay them or anything."

Nakili swiped a tuna on rye, observing, "I can see this party planning's gonna be tons of fun, fun, fun! You and Dana, man, you two are too much! You gonna butt heads over every last detail?"

Rockett opened her mouth to protest, but Nakili playfully punched her arm. "Forget it, I was kidding. This'll work out. It's all good."

As the girls snaked their way through the crowded

lunchroom back to their table, Nakili stopped to trade quick "heys" with a bunch of people. Which is when it hit Rockett: Nakili may not be a One, but she is what popular is all about, someone genuinely liked by so many different people.

Viva Cortez tapped her arm to say, "Thanks for the note you sent." Arrow waved, and Chaz Franklin, studly bud of Cleve's, said, "Yo, Nakili, give me a shout-out after school. I have to ask you something." Arnold Zeitbaum, their grade's most awkward, and okay, strange, kid, said, "Kudos on your science fair submission. I salute you!" Even Sharla Norvell, best known for who she didn't like — everyone, mostly! — shot Nakili a friendly smile.

I bet Nakili's going to invite, like, all these people to this party. Who should I suggest? Rockett grinned at Jessie as she passed by her usual table. *Well, Jessie, for sure — and I'll definitely see that Darnetta gets an invite. And maybe . . . just 'cause I know Jessie sorta kinda likes Max Diamond — even though I have no idea what she sees in the little scamp — I'll see about getting him on the list. That'll show Jessie I'm totally thinking of her.*

By the time Nakili and Rockett returned to their table, Dana and Ginger were halfway done eating. Dana had pulled out a magazine and the two were huddling over it. Miko wasn't included.

Nakili took care of that — or tried to. Biting into her lunch, she casually remarked, "So I never asked you, Miko, who'd you trump in the chess tournament this time?"

Nakili never found out.

Later, Rockett would realize that Miko probably wasn't even going to answer. Which accounted for her looking away at the moment of impact.

A moment that arrived punctuated by a bloodcurdling scream. Dana's sound-barrier-shattering shrieks were accompanied by frantically pulling something off her head. Something that had smashed into hundreds of sharp, pointed little white pieces, and left a gooey stream of thick, yellow-streaked translucent glop tangled in her hair.

An egg. Classification: in its precooked stage. Also known as: raw.

Instantly, every kid — every teacher, every hair-netted cafeteria aide — spun around to find out what the commotion was. As if a giant magnet had been placed squarely on Dana's head instead of an egg, a rubbernecking crowd moved as one toward her for a better view.

What they saw was a dripping Dana, who continued to howl while swiping egg gunk out of her eyes and off her face. Of course, her frantic antics only made it worse.

"I'm gonna annihilate whoever did this!" Dana thundered.

"Me too!" Nakili, who'd already grabbed a bunch of napkins to start wiping up, angrily vowed, while commanding Ginger to get more napkins.

"Who is responsible for this?" Mr. Baldus, one of the teachers on caf duty, demanded as he and Mr. Pill, who came running out from behind the food counter, dashed over to Dana.

Unsurprisingly, no one copped to the prank.

Mr. Baldus was Rockett's homeroom teacher, and usually, a kind of funny guy who was never in a bad — or even serious — mood. He was always up for a joke, with one major exception: when it was played on someone. And this qualified, big-time.

Baldus started to help Dana up from the table, as Nakili tried to contain the dripping egg. Scowling, he shouted, "Someone threw this. And someone — maybe a lot of you — saw it. Someone better 'fess up — now!"

Was it Rockett's face that betrayed her? For, as bad luck would have it, just as the egg had flown through the air, she had been looking around the room — innocently thinking of who else she could suggest for the invitee list.

And her eyes had been trained on a certain boy. A boy whose arm was still poised in a pitching position, because he had, in fact, just released a small white oval projectile.

What Dana saw, as she allowed Nakili and Mr. Baldus to help her away from the table, was the horrified expression on Rockett's face.

Immediately, she suspected.

At the top of her lungs, she bellowed, "Rockett saw who did it! She did! I know it! You better tell, Rockett!"

Silence descended on the cafeteria, way more disconcerting than Dana's thunderbolts. All eyes turned to

Rockett, who turned tomato red. It was as if everyone in the caf held a collective breath, waiting to see if Rockett would reveal the culprit.

Mr. Pill barked, "If you saw it, say it!"

Mr. Baldus stepped in. In a gentle tone, he inquired, "Did you, Rockett?"

Tell me this isn't happening! How can I tell what I saw? But how can I . . . not? Oh, Ruben! Why do you have to be such a juvie brat sometimes? Especially when other times, you're so amazingly cool? Why can't you just be one way? I know you'll totally hate me if I tell on you. But Dana will never forgive me if I don't. And . . . this time she'd be right. Nakili would know it, too. That I was too chicken to tell the truth — that I let this sorta-crush get in the way of everything. But I like being your friend. And I know I'll lose that if I give you up. I could just say I didn't see who did it. I could make Dana believe that. Couldn't I?

CHAPTER THREE

"I saw who did it."

Rockett whirled around, shocked. The speaker? In a quiet, but self-assured tone, it was Miko.

Mr. Baldus eyed the girls warily. After a moment's pause, he said, "Why don't both of you come with me to Principal Herrera's office." He checked around the cafeteria again, stern-faced. "Unless whoever did this has decided to speak up. Confession, I remind you, is good for the soul. And if you don't buy that, try this: By not coming forward, you put these two girls on the spot. A massively unboss thing to do."

His request was met with a combination of stifled giggles . . . and silence. Until, that is, Dana spoke up. As Nakili and Ginger, armed with a pile of paper towels, escorted her to the girls' locker room for a shower and shampoo, she snarled, "Rockett, if you protect little crush-boy now, you are so in for it!"

Oh, no! How could she shout that out, in front of the whole school? Now what'll I do?

"She'll do the right thing!" Nakili growled, mostly for Dana's benefit, but loud enough so half the room heard her.

Rockett gulped.

Miko grimaced.

Baldus motioned. "Come with me."

Wordlessly, Rockett and Miko grabbed their backpacks and marched behind Mr. Baldus down the corridor that led to the principal's office. With each step, Rockett imagined asking Miko not to say anything. No real damage was done, after all. It was just a harmless egg-beaning.

But Miko never even turned toward her, so Rockett would have had to grab her arm and stop her. Which, as they walked through the doors to the outer area of the main office, she couldn't bring herself to do.

"Wait here, girls." Mr. Baldus pointed to the benches against the wall, as he asked the dark-haired secretary, Mrs. Hoffman, "Is Principal H in her chambers?"

Mrs. Hoffman replied, "She is, but she's in serious conference with one of our students."

Serious conference. Rockett and Miko knew what that meant: Someone was in trouble. Of the Capital T kind.

And someone else was about to be. That was the reason they were there. To squeal on Ruben. Mr. Baldus knocked on the door of Mrs. Herrera's private office. Summoned inside, he closed it behind him.

Miko turned to Rockett. "I'm really sorry. I know you like Ruben —"

Rockett felt a sudden surge of annoyance. She interrupted, "It's okay. He did it. Dana suspects it. We saw it. End of story."

Miko squirmed, obviously uncomfortable. She lowered her voice. "Look, if telling on him will totally mess up your relationship, then, we could . . . um . . . say we *thought* we saw who did it. But, now we realize we didn't. Exactly. See who did it. That is."

What is going on here? Did an alien steal Miko's body? Okay, so Miko's been acting strange lately. But one thing you can count on is Miko playing by the rules. Now she's suggesting we fib?

Rockett's eyes widened in surprise. "I can't believe you just said that."

Miko set her jaw. "Why not?"

"Well, it just seems kinda unlike you, that's all."

"Because I'm always 'ultra do right girl'? That's what you think of me."

Rockett flushed and shifted uncomfortably on the bench. "Hold on. We're friends, remember? I know you."

"Do you, Rockett?"

Before she could respond, Mr. Baldus bounded out of the principal's office and straight up to the girls. "Okey-dokey, ladies. Here's the pooper-scoop. As soon as Mrs. Herrera is done in there with our delinquent du jour, she'll call you in. I looped her into the situation. Now, I'm going to head back to the scene of the crime. Who knows? Maybe we'll all be lucky and someone will have rethought his or her decision to trade cowardly for courageous."

When Baldus was gone, Rockett took a deep breath.

She so did not want to even ponder Miko's "do you really know me" question. So she changed the subject. "Wonder who's in there with Herrera?"

Miko yawned. "What's the dif?"

Rockett guessed, "Probably Bo Pezanski. That boy's always in trouble for something."

"Unlike others who are never in trouble . . . like me, right?"

Okay, that's it! I've had enough. Unlike Dana and Nakili, I am not letting her blow me off. "Miko, what exactly is going on? Why are you acting like this?"

"Like what?" Miko scowled.

Rockett had never, ever seen her friend so . . . confrontational. Usually, Miko was sweet, even-tempered — agreeable.

Just then, the door to Mrs. Herrera's office opened. And out popped . . . Cleve? Rockett stared.

Cleve's the one in trouble? Now, this is a first! Correction: This is a day for firsts — weird firsts. Okay, I know his grades haven't exactly been stellar, but . . . unless he's, like, being expelled or something, you don't usually get called in for that. Unless he's in trouble for something else . . . ? But what? Cleve's like Mr. All-Around Whistling Pines.

Rockett was about to turn to Miko to see if she shared her shock, but what came next threw her for an even bigger loop. Cleve, who should've been fully freaked out after the serious conference session, took one look at Miko and lit up. He headed straight over.

"Yo, Meeks, wussup? When Baldus barged in, he said

24

two students were here to give the low-down on some chaos in the cafeteria. Don't tell me you're in the middle of it?"

Miko, who'd been all-chill exactly one moment ago, was suddenly all-flirty. She giggled. "Not exactly: just an unexpected incident to report on."

Cleve grinned. "Yeah, those unexpected incidents, man, they'll get ya every time. Well, I hope yours goes better than mine did. But, uh . . ." He stopped and eyed Rockett, as if deciding whether to continue. Then, he leaned in toward Miko and squeezed her arm. "So, later? Same time, same place?"

Miko bit her lip, trying to hide a smile. Unsuccessfully.

Rockett fumbled her attempt to wrap *that* strange encounter around her brain. Just then, Mrs. Herrera's large, square frame appeared in the doorway. "Mr. Goodstaff!" she reprimanded. "Did I not just tell you to get to class — no dawdling! Your charm may work with the girls, but not with me. I will get to the bottom of this. Count on it."

As Cleve dutifully dashed out the door, Mrs. Herrera gestured to Rockett and Miko. "You're up, ladies. Come on in."

Miko and Rockett took the seats facing Herrera's imposing wood desk. Their principal shook her head. "It never rains, it pours. This must be my day for discipline cases. So what exactly did happen in the lunchroom? Mr. Baldus informs me you girls witnessed everything."

Rockett cleared her throat and focused on her shoes. *Am I really going to do this?*

Miko gripped the side of her chair.

Mrs. Herrera sensed their discomfort. "Look, ladies, I know it feels awkward to squeal on one of your classmates. I understand your hesitation."

"What will happen . . . to the person . . . who did it?" Rockett asked quietly. "It won't be that bad, right? I mean, it was just a silly prank. It wasn't like anyone got hurt."

"This time. That's the key, Rockett. No one got hurt, just embarrassed. But what disturbs me more than anything is that no one came forward to confess. And worse, even, with the exception of you two, everyone else who saw it participated in the cover-up. So where will this behavior lead if we let it go? If there are no repercussions, the next time someone could throw a fork, or a knife, and then what? Next time, someone *could* get hurt."

Argument-proof, that one.

"The guilty party," Mrs. H continued, "will get detention. That's a given. His or her parents may be called in. He or she will have to apologize to Dana, and do something to make it up to her. Other than that, I will make sure the whole school knows about the punishment. There must be a deterrent to this kind of disruptive behavior. So . . . ?"

Rockett and Miko exchanged nervous glances. Though they obviously hadn't planned it, they said it in sync: "Ruben Rosales."

*   *   *

26

"I feel like the world's biggest tattletale," Rockett mumbled glumly as she and Miko left Mrs. Herrera's office.

"Doesn't feel so good, does it?" Miko sounded like she was challenging her.

"Well," Rockett said, "I guess I probably would have felt worse if I didn't tell. Especially since Dana was the target."

Miko shook her head. "This whole thing is lose/lose. You tell the truth — 'cause everyone *knows* that's the right thing to do," she said sarcastically, "and where does it get you? You make enemies. If you lie, you feel worse."

Impulsively, Rockett tapped Miko's shoulder. "Hey, look. I don't know exactly what's going on, and . . . it's cool if you don't want to tell me. But just so you know, Miko? I'm here for you."

Miko sighed. "Everything's cool, Rockett. Catch you later."

Everything's cool, Rockett? Nuh-uh! Everything's totally bizarro-world. Miko's like, metamorphosing into someone else. First she suggests we lie about Ruben. And then there's the Cleve thing. Potentially much huger. 'Cause I was half-kidding before, but I was right: Miko's crushing on Cleve. And . . . he's . . . reciprocating? Didn't he just say, "Later, same time, same place?" What other proof do I need? I have to tell Nakili. This is huge!

27

Confession Session

Oh, man! How did this happen? It's like Herrera has X-ray vision! She thinks she busted me, so I better think fast about how I'm gettin' outta this one! At least this new sitch with Miko is working out better than imagined! Despite what people say, that girl has layers.
Labels! What am I, a can of soup? They make me totally . . . urrrgh . . . I don't know, boil or something! Are you the person you are, because everyone gives you that label? Miko-the-brainiac. Miko-the-winner. Miko-the-do-the-right-thing-girl. Sometimes I wish people would say something else about me!

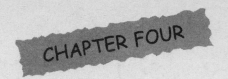

CHAPTER FOUR

"Pssst, pass it down. Miko Kajiyama likes Cleve Good-staff!"

Rockett cringed as she heard the words — her words, meant only for Nakili's ears — bounced around like a beach ball, all the way down the line of girls stretched out on the gym floor doing stomach crunches.

Wait! That's not what I said! She wanted to bolt up and shout across the room, but in fact, that's exactly what she'd said. She just hadn't meant for the entire world to get wind of it!

Rockett had been bursting to tell Nakili what she'd witnessed between Cleve and Miko, but after the Herrera visit, she hadn't been able to get her friend alone. She decided against passing a note in one of her afternoon classes, just in case Dana, or worse, Nicole, intercepted. But the main thing was to tell Nakili when Miko wasn't around.

Then came PE, the perfect opportunity. Miko had left early to go to a chess club competition. And in PE, you didn't need to pass notes.

It wasn't like Rockett didn't try to corner Nakili in the locker room before they got out on the gym floor. Only that's where Dana had chosen to corner *Rockett*. As the girls were changing into their gym shorts, Dana had sidled up to her, demanding, "So, Rockett, rumor has it that you gave up little crush-boy after all, and told Mrs. Herrera who the bad guy was. Gospel?"

Rockett had stared at her. "Do you always have to be such an irritator-tot?" She clenched her teeth. "I saw Ruben do it. And that's what I said. Happy now?"

"Not really," Dana muttered, and stalked away.

Just then the bell rang, signaling the start of the period.

Phys ed always began with warm-up exercises: Since she and Nakili were spotting each other during stomach crunches, Rockett saw it as, finally, her chance to spill. In a hushed, sorta private way.

So, on an upward curl, as Nakili was holding her ankles, Rockett whispered, "I was right. About Miko and Cleve."

Nakili, not fully hearing her, echoed — just a little too loud — "*What's* up with Miko and Cleve?"

Rockett had to wait until she came up for the next curl. "She *is* crushing on him! I found out in Herrera's office."

Nakili scoffed. "No way! Girlfriend would never give Goodstaff the time of day."

Again, Rockett had to wait until she was up again. This time, she held the curl long enough to repeat, almost word for word, what had been exchanged between

Miko and Cleve in the principal's outer office — adding that it seemed the attraction was mutual. She finished with, "I think we should keep this little secret to ourselves."

Nakili should have been rendered speechless. It was, after all, a kind of bombshell. Only instead of pressing the "mute" button, it was like Nakili accidentally hit "volume up" instead. 'Cause what came out was way louder than it should have been. "So you're sayin' Miko's into Cleve? And he's into her right back?"

And so it spread around the gym. And there was nothing Rockett could do to stop it.

By the time the period was over, the entire girls' locker room was abuzz. Whenever Rockett tried to stem the tide, she was put on the spot and drilled for details. That only dug her in even deeper.

By dismissal, the Miko-Cleve "this-just-in" bulletin might as well have been posted on the walls and announced over the PA system. The only two people in the school who hadn't heard it were the subjects themselves: Miko, gone, and Cleve, who had left early, too, though no one knew exactly why.

Judging by the excited ripples around the school, most kids were mega-amused by the news and reacted with variations of "You're kidding!"

Nicole Whittaker was not one of those kids. At the top of the stairwell, she cornered Rockett. Pointing a manicured, sparkly nail at Rockett's chin, Nicole challenged, "Word has it that you started this rumor. Which, for your four-one-one, is ridiculous."

Rockett remained silent. *What can I say? How about . . . nothing? I don't have to answer her.*

Whatever. It was a rhetorical question anyway.

But Nicole's glacial facial sent a chill through Rockett. She declared, "Rumors are only interesting if there's a shred of truth to them. I should know. You, on the other hand, are obviously a novice at this. Allow me to educate you. You end up looking lame when you start a rumor that doesn't have even the possibility of accuracy. It's worse when everyone can see right through it."

Again Rockett was silent.

Again Nicole didn't care. "Well, if you can stand to hear the truth, here it is. Maybe shrimpy little Miko thinks she can get Cleve to pay attention to her. But that would only last as long as the homework she lets him copy. Cleve could never, ever be interested in her in any other way. I know him best. So I'd say you are guilty of spreading a total falsehood. And if you don't want to make things worse for yourself socially — though I'm not sure how that could happen! — you should take it back right now."

Finally, Rockett reacted. "Is there going to be an intermission? 'Cause I'm not sure I can wait. Here's the deal, Nicole. I wasn't trying to spread a rumor. Unlike some people . . ." She paused for what she hoped was effect. "I'm not about that."

"Trying or not, Rockett, that's exactly what you did.

And I demand you find a way to hit 'undo.' By tomorrow morning, I want you to let the whole school know you were so sadly mistaken. Or I do it for you. Your call."

She demands? Excuse me? She's not the boss of me! And besides, this has nothing to do with her! How dare she threaten me! No matter how crummy I feel that the whole school overheard me give away Miko's secret, no way will I cave to Her Nastiness!

Rockett drew a sharp breath. "I owe you nothing, Nicole, least of all any kind of explanation. But I am no liar. I don't start rumors. I know what I saw and what I heard. And one more thing: I am *too through* with you!"

On that, Rockett meant to stalk away, but Nicole snagged the last word. "You know what, Rockett? You put the *duh* in deluded."

Steaming, Rockett barreled over to the Birdcage, the indoor gazebo just near the entrance to Whistling Pines. That's where everyone gathered in the morning and in the afternoon to wait for the bus. Now, at the end of the day, it was wall-to-wall kids.

Rockett brushed by them all, busting in on Nakili and Dana, who were midconvo.

"I can't believe the nerve of Nicole!" Rockett sputtered.

Nakili spun around. "Whattup? Did that girl slice 'n' dice you or something?"

A prospect that clearly amused Dana, judging by the sudden upturn at the corners of her mouth.

Seething, Rockett replayed the encounter, concluding, "I don't even care that she called me a liar and threatened me. She acts like she owns Cleve or something!"

Dana tilted her head and touched her chin with her forefinger. "Let me guess. Your middle name is Scientist! 'Cause, Rockett-girl, you finally figured it out. In Nicole's mind, she *does* own Cleve!"

Rockett Scientist, like she hadn't heard *that* one before! "Whatever. But the way she talks about Miko! She totally dissed her. She actually came out and said that Cleve could never be interested in her."

Nakili shook her head, unconvinced. "I'm having a hard time with another thing, too. Cleve represents everything Miko can't stand. The boy's full of himself, a full-on flirt. He never listens to what you say, 'cause he's so busy talkin' about himself."

"Still," Dana mused, with a conciliatory nod, "Rockett saw and heard it in Herrera's office. And wasn't our lesson of the day that Rockett *does* call 'em as she sees 'em — even when it means incriminating her boyfriend? Hence, this Miko-Cleve thing must be true!"

Rockett glared. "Gee, thanks, Dana. Only the next time you're reaching for a compliment, try it front-handed!"

Nakili ignored the swipes between her friends. She shook her head adamantly. "I'm not sayin' *did* it happen? I'm asking why? And, if Miko does have a thing for Cleve — even if it's temporary insanity — why wouldn't she tell us?"

Dana shrugged. "It's like I said before. Maybe Miko doesn't feel she can confide in us anymore. Maybe, I don't know, she really does feel abandoned by her CSG sisters."

"Abandoned? No way!" Nakili stomped, forcing Dana to jerk her head up and Rockett to jump. "That makes negative sense!"

Rockett interjected. "Or at least as much sense as Miko and Cleve!"

"Okay," Nakili finally conceded. "I'm still not down with this, but if it *is* true, we gotta get on the party train now and set things right. Actions speak louder, girlfriends, and if we can't talk to Miko about our friendship, we gotta show her. Soon as I get home, I'm gonna call the rec room, see if the date's available, and book it."

Dana sighed. "I don't know if a party's the answer, N, but after I baby-sit Rachel, I'll start making up the guest list. I'll e-mail it to you."

Rockett offered, "I could design the invitations. I assume you want them, since it's a surprise party."

The sound of the school bus horn interrupted their convo. "That's my wheels," noted Dana as she craned her neck to see outside. "Why don't we talk about this later? Call me, Nakili!"

Just before dashing out, she called over her shoulder, "You, too, Rockett."

Nakili grinned and waved. "Eyes on the prize, that's the spirit. We each do one thing to get this party rolling."

Focusing on the invitations was all it took to switch Rockett's mood from enraged to engaged. With ideas for colors and clever wording dancing in her head, she was just about to get on the bus, when someone tapped her on the shoulder.

Rockett whirled around. Instinctively, she lit up.

The boy whose finger remained on her shoulder usually had a smile on his lips and a twinkle in his eye. That sparkle was one of the things Rockett liked most about him.

But there was no luster around Ruben Rosales that moment. His dark eyes were clouded, his lips pressed together grimly.

And Rockett got nervous. *He hasn't talked to me all day. Now he's gonna confront me about the lunchroom thing.*

Ruben got right to it. "I heard a rumor, new girl."

Whew! He just wants to know about Miko! Relieved, Rockett blurted, "You mean about Miko and Cleve? How unbelievable is that . . . ?"

"Not that one." Ruben, a man on a mission, was not about to be distracted.

And Rockett knew it. She didn't really have to listen, because she knew what he was going to ask her.

"Look, I know I messed up with the egg thing. Me and Max were just having a friendly little catch. If he'd *caught* it, none of this would have happened. It was dumb and I'm gonna get crowned for it. But here's what I don't know. Rumor's raging that *you* gave me up to Herrera. Only, I'm not so sure about that. See, here's how *I* think it went down. . . ."

Rockett swallowed hard.

Ruben continued. "You saw me, I know that. And you had to go to Herrera's office so Dana wouldn't dismember you! But you went with Miko, who also saw me. And her, man! Everyone knows she's genetically incapable of lying — the girl can't help herself. So she's the one who probably spilled it and you were just there, an innocent bystander. 'Cause you and me, *chica*, we're friends, right? And friends don't give up friends . . . especially over a little egg toss."

Rockett stiffened but didn't say a word.

Ruben continued, "So anyway, I'm busted. Herrera called home and I gotta wait here till my pops comes for me. Nothin's gonna change that. And I'm not about revenge or anything. I'm not even gonna say anything to Miko. What would be the point? But I gotta know who my friends are. So tell me the rumor's bogus — it was *her*, right, not you? You and me, new girl, we're cool?"

Rockett chewed on a fingernail and looked away.

He's leading me right into this! I'll just nod and let him think it wasn't me. How easy would that be? Miko won't find out. He's not even going to ask her. If I let him believe what he already does, he won't be mad at me. But . . . I'll know I lied. And how stinky will that feel? Why did he even put me in this position in the first place? Baldus was right: If he were honorable, he would have confessed right away. Maybe he's not even worth being friends with. But . . . look at him. There's so much more beneath the clown-boy surface. I don't want him to think I betrayed him.

Confession Session

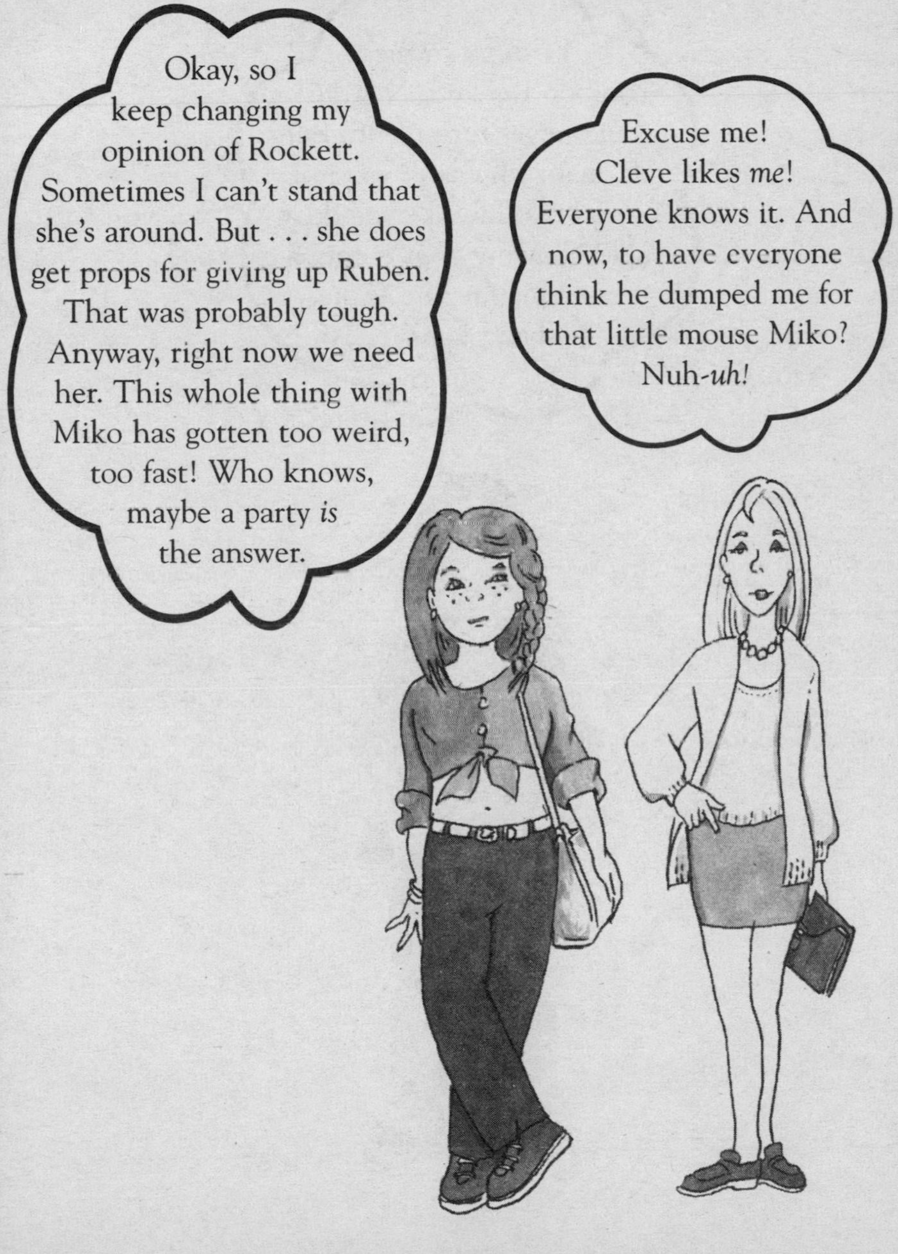

CHAPTER FIVE

Rockett held her breath, then slowly exhaled. "Miko," she mumbled to Ruben, then — eyes focused on the ground — paused, still conflicted over whether to finish the sentence truthfully: *and I, we both told on you.*

She waited a second to continue. But that split second was enough.

Eyes twinkling now, Ruben held up his hand. "Slap me five, new girl. I knew you wouldn't go all stoolie on me. No matter *what* other people say. You and me have a kind of connection, right?"

Rockett swallowed hard. The smile she attempted was phony.

Ruben knew it, too, but he misinterpreted the reason. "No worries. When it comes to Miko, my lips are sealed."

"You won't tell her . . . what I kind of . . . said?"

He made a zip-lock motion across his mouth. "No reason to. The damage is done. I just had to know the truth. Later, *chica.*" In a flash, he was gone.

Rockett's emotions spiraled like a paper airplane in a nosedive. Miko's words boomeranged: *You tell the truth, you make enemies. You lie, you feel worse.* Just to avoid Ruben's wrath, she'd lied to him — which made her good friend such the cheese: a stand-alone tattletale. *Miko won't find out?* That made her feel better — not at all. She talked to no one the entire bus ride home.

Rockett's father had sharp daughter-radar. It was in full effect, the minute she came home. Instead of his usual cheery "Look who's here!" he said softly, "Hey, kiddo, what's wrong? You look like you just lost your best friend."

Rockett wanted to blurt, "No, that happened when we moved here." But that would've been a knee-jerk reaction — faux, to boot. Instead, she went with a deep sigh. "I'm fine."

She wasn't. And he knew it. He came over and gave her a peck on the cheek. "Want to talk about it? Maybe over a dish of ice cream?" It was one of Rockett's father's theories — and, as an inventor, he had many — that ice cream was invented to soothe life's little problems.

Usually, Rockett agreed. Not today. "Thanks but no thanks, Dad. I'm just gonna head upstairs. I have to start designing something."

That reminded him. Her dad snapped his fingers. "Speaking of designing, guess who called?"

Rockett didn't need to buy a vowel. He had to mean the family's reigning designing diva: Rockett's older sister, Juno, an amazingly talented Web artist who was away at college.

"That's great, Dad. What's up with her?" Rockett was

only mildly interested. She loved her big sis, natch, but the day's events at school weighed massively.

"She called with good news. She's been nominated for an art award. Only she'd planned to come home the week they're announced. So now she's trying to figure out what to do."

"Well, if she calls again, tell her I said good luck." *Not that she needs it. Awards and Juno go together like . . . well, awards and Miko!*

That thought launched Rockett up the steps — straight to her room and the computer, where inspiration came fast and furiously. Within an hour she had a dozen designs for Miko's invitations. The thought didn't escape Rockett that her creativity spurt was fueled by guilt. Like she could make up for the lie she just told Ruben with killer designs for Miko.

Pushing that thought out of her head, she narrowed the potential invites to three:

Under a drawing of a sombrero, she'd written, "Ssssh! Keep it under your hat. Join Miko's friends for a super-secret surprise party!"

The second one was, "It's a secret! It's a surprise! It's a celebration of the sweetest, smartest babe in the nabe, our friend Miko!"

The third was maybe the cleverest. On the front, she wrote, "Can you keep a secret? The amazing Miko is arty-smarty, so come one, come all, let's party hearty!"

Rockett had just e-mailed her designs to Nakili when

43

the little beep that signaled an instant message went off.

Assuming it was Dana with the invitee list, Rockett was stoked. A feeling that fizzled immediately when her on-line buddy turned out to be Mavis Wartella-DePew, self-proclaimed psychic.

Mavis was the kind of girl who put the *irk* in quirky. A total oddball — and proud of it!

She had written an "urgent" message. "Rockett! You didn't talk to me all day. And I have something important to tell you!"

Most people at school avoided Mavis. Who wanted to hang with someone beyond uncool? But Mavis had really been nice to Rockett, especially in those scary first few days when she'd been new at school. Besides, Rockett wasn't most people. She immediately responded, "Sorry, Mavis. It was not my best day! To the max!"

Encouraged, Mavis wrote back, "I could have told you that, if you'd taken a few seconds to talk to me. Anyway, Rockett, I feel a tingling in my jawbone. And you know what that signals!"

As a joke, Rockett wrote, "You were contacted by aliens?"

Mavis ignored Rockett's flip response. She took her seer status very seriously. "It signals, Rockett, that all is not what it seems. I refer to the rumor. The Miko and Cleve thing. You have entered the weirdo zone with that one."

Rockett scratched her head. Mavis and Nicole sure

had different ways of expressing themselves — but essentially, they were saying the same thing. As if this day could get any weirder!

"Well, I know what I saw," Rockett responded, adding, "gotta go now. See you tomorrow."

But Mavis wouldn't click off. She wrote, "Miko's going through some stuff, Rockett. It has nothing to do with Cleve."

In spite of herself, Rockett replied, "What stuff? What do you know?"

The return message, "Just trust me," made Rockett roll her eyes. *Why I would even think for one minute that Mavis knows anything — that's the real mystery!*

A few minutes later, Rockett's nine-year-old brother, Jasper — all splotchy freckles and carrot-red hair — blasted into her room with a this-just-in. "Jessie's here!"

Rockett whirled around, surprised. She had no plans with Jessie. "Tell her to come up, Jas."

Jasper wrinkled his nose. "What am I, your slave? Tell her yourself."

Rockett tilted her head. "Tell her and I'll play a video game with you later."

Jasper considered — for a split second. Rockett hadn't hung out with him in a long time. "Deal."

A few seconds later, Jessie's freckled face appeared in the doorway. She was a little flushed: She must have biked over.

"Hey, Jess, cool surprise. What's up?" Rockett greeted, motioning her to come in.

45

Jessie explained, "I tried to call, but your line's been busy."

"I've kinda been on the computer all afternoon," Rockett replied. "Sorry!"

"No big, I just wanted to talk to you. Got a second?"

As they usually did, the girls settled cross-legged on Rockett's bed, facing each other.

"So what's the nine-one-one, Jess?"

Jessie tilted her head. "I just want to be sure everything's okay. That you're not mad at me or anything?"

"Why would I be mad at you?"

She shrugged. "I've been trying to think of a reason all day. You've been avoiding me, that's all."

Rockett's jaw dropped. *Just because I didn't sit with her at lunch — and okay — and I guess, uh, didn't really talk to her during PE . . . but just for that, she thinks I'm mad? Sheesh! Sometimes I forget that she's super-sensitive.*

"I wasn't avoiding you, Jess. Other stuff just came up, and I kinda got, you know, sidetracked."

"Stuff you don't want to tell me about?" Jessie probed gently.

It unnerved Rockett. So, guiltily, she told her how Nakili and Dana were wiggin' about Miko. And that they'd decided to throw her a party. Which accounted for Rockett being in the CSG lunch-bunch today.

Jessie brightened. "It's awesome that you guys are doing something cool for Miko."

Rockett added, "You'll be invited, of course."

"It's okay. You don't have to say that."

"No, really. I'm not just saying it. I was on the computer all afternoon designing invitations and . . ." Rockett paused, not wanting to come out and say she'd seen the list.

Jessie let it go. She had something else on her mind. "Whatever. Look, there's other stuff I wanted to ask you about — so many rumors are floating! Everyone's saying that you told on Ruben. Did you?"

Rockett turned away so Jessie wouldn't see her flush. "Hmmm, I'd rather not go there, if it's all the same to you, Jessie. What else?"

Jessie, stung that Rockett wasn't sharing with her, continued, "The big rumor that's going around the school. About Miko and Cleve. Is it really true? I mean, everyone's saying you started it."

Rockett took a deep breath and got up off the bed. "You know what, Jess? I better not say anything else. My big mouth got me into enough trouble today."

Hurt now clouded Jessie's face. "Okay. I guess you just don't want to tell me. I guess this time you don't need my advice or anything."

Nailed! Rockett felt like she'd just taken a soccer ball to the stomach. So often Rockett had come running to Jessie for help . . . she was the go-to girl for secret sharing. *Was* being the operative word. Present tense, Jessie wasn't letting her off the hook.

"Busted, Jess. You're right, I haven't been the best

kind of friend today. Forgive me?" Rockett walked back over to the bed, a pleading look on her face.

Jessie shook her head. "Sure, Rockett. It's okay."

Rockett tried harder. "Just . . . hey, anyway, I'm pretty sure Darnetta's invited. To Miko's surprise party, that is."

Amused at Rockett's attempt to console her, Jessie teased, "How can you get people invited? Are you like an honorary CSG now?"

Riled, Rockett retorted, "No, of course not. I'm just helping them with the party. Speaking of which, do you want to see if Max will be invited?"

Okay, so that was a little dig — but just to get back at her for that "are you a CSG now?" thing. Jessie won't admit it, but she's crushing on the creep.

Flustered, Jessie blushed. "I know you don't like him. And even though I kind of once did, I'm over it. Still, he's not so obnoxious. Everyone has a nice side."

That night, Rockett had the weirdest dream. It was about a note that got passed around in class. She'd started it, innocently enough. She'd written, "I think Mavis looks tired today." She'd meant to pass it to Jessie, but it got intercepted by Nicole. She'd added something to it. "She's really sick!" Then Nicole passed it to Whitney, who'd written, "With a deadly disease!" With each person, Rockett got more and more upset. She kept trying to get up and stop it — to say, "Wait, that's not what I meant!" But no words would come out.

Rockett woke in a cold sweat. Before getting out of bed, she reached over to the phone and called Nakili. The minute her friend picked up, Rockett blurted, "I need to talk to you!"

Nakili responded with a yawn. "Down, girl. I barely got my eyes open."

"Sorry, I just had this dream. And it kinda spooked me."

"Eyes wide open now. Dream-interpretation service is open for business."

Rockett grunted. "This dream needs no interpretation. It was beyond obvious. It was about a rumor . . . that took on a life of its own. And came out all twisted on the other side. The Miko and Cleve thing, I so didn't mean to start . . ."

Nakili sighed. "I'm with you in the doghouse, yelling it out like that. I was just so stunned, I don't know what came over me."

"Yeah, well, true or not, I feel bad about it. And right now, it's like Miko and Cleve are the only ones who haven't heard it."

"Can't be. This is the info age, girl. Trust me, by now they know."

"Well, do you think I should, like, apologize or something? Or think of a way to stop it?"

"You can apologize — we both can. But it won't do any good. We can't stop a rumor like this once it's started. Only Miko and Cleve can."

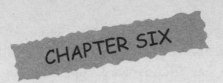

CHAPTER SIX

Curiously, they didn't.

Not because they hadn't heard it, either.

Nakili was right. By the time Rocket arrived at school the next day, the subjects of the rumor obviously knew all about it. Word was Cleve had come home to a dozen messages on his answering machine. Half were from his buddy Max, wigged that Cleve was "holding out on him." The other half were from Nicole. *Wigged* wasn't the word for her. *Rabid,* as in "beyond," nailed it.

That Cleve had returned no calls severely fractured them both.

Miko had not received any calls that night. But she'd barely gotten to her locker the next morning when several people descended on her. Rockett saw Viva Cortez elbow her jokingly. "Hey, soccer friend, now I know why the sudden interest in our boys' team!"

Miko looked up, surprised, but only smiled.

Arrow Mayfield, who was walking with Viva, clucked, "Cleve Goodstaff, huh? I always thought that boy took self-absorption to a cosmic level, but maybe I was wrong . . . right?"

This time, Miko giggled.

*   *   *

Cleve was treating the whole thing in the same unconcerned way. Max was in his face all during homeroom, but he'd just smiled his lazy Cleve smile and changed the subject. When Chaz tried to get the scoop, Cleve reversed the tease by putting *him* on the spot. In a stage whisper meant to be overheard by half the class, Cleve went, "Everyone says you like Stephanie. Or is it Nakili today? Maybe Ginger?"

It worked. Chaz — along with all three girls mentioned — totally squirmed, faced forward suddenly, furiously focusing on the blackboard.

What truly impressed Rockett, however, was how Cleve "handled" Nicole. To head off her wrath, Cleve aimed at her ego. Naturally athletic, he was a good shot, too. He mentioned how diesel she looked in her designer khakis, "just like those magazine models." Nicole tossed her head back theatrically at that. Then, as the bell rang, he called out, "Yo, Whittaker, buzz you later. We'll hang."

Mission: Pacification. Accomplished.

While marveling over Cleve's spin control, Rockett was also painfully aware of something else: Ruben's absence. *Is he sick? Or tardy? He couldn't be suspended or anything, could he? Herrera said he'd get detention, not suspension.*

That's what was on her mind when Nicole purposely sideswiped her in the corridor after homeroom. "Lucky for you Cleve cleared this up," the haughty One said. "You don't want to know what could happen to a certain someone who spreads ugly rumors."

51

Rockett retorted, "No, I wouldn't want to take that crown away from you!"

And so the morning went. As if by secret pact to "neither deny nor confirm," both Miko and Cleve remained totally tight-lipped about the rumor. Which, whether or not it was true, was really out of character — for both of them!

The closest thing to a confrontation came just before lunch, in the girls' room. Rockett and Miko were washing up when Whitney Weiss walked in, announcing, "I refuse to believe this ridiculous rumor. I get that Miko here is taking the high road and not commenting, but if I were her, I'd refute this in the school newspaper. We should stop vicious rumors before they go any further."

If Miko was about to respond, she never got the chance. For at that second, Nicole blasted out of a stall, full fury ahead. Glaring at Miko and Rockett, she snarled, "Excellent idea, Whitney! The rumor is bogus. Everyone in homeroom heard Cleve ask *me* out."

No, Nicole, everyone in homeroom heard Cleve do damage control. Saying he might call you is not the same as asking you out!

Unfazed, Miko shrugged. "Did the school newspaper start a gossip column?"

Miko didn't have lunch with her friends. She told Rockett about "another commitment" during that period.

"You sure, Miko?" Rockett had asked. "You're not trip-ping about this whole rumor mess?"

If Rockett thought that would lead Miko to unload about Cleve, she was wrong. For all Miko said was, "Are you kidding? Why should I care what certain people are saying about me? I really have elsewhere to be, that's all. See you in afternoon classes."

Since Miko's lunchtime no-show handed the party planners a chance to discuss the invites and the list, Nakili asked Rockett to definitely sit with her and Dana.

Before agreeing, Rockett went up to her usual table, where Jessie, Mavis, and Darnetta were, and mentioned her decision to sit with the CSGs for one more day.

Jessie pretended not to care. "I understand. Do what you have to."

Mavis added, "Just remember what I told you, Rockett."

Darnetta said nothing.

With a shrug, Rockett walked back over to the CSG table. On the way, she scanned the lunchroom to see if Ruben had shown up — she hadn't seen him all day.

On a whim, she sidetracked to the table he usually sat at, alongside his friend Wolf DuBois. Wolf was a really cool boy Rockett had gotten to know a whole lot better during a school trip last month.

"What's the good word?" Rockett greeted him.

Wolf looked up from the magazine he was reading and shot her a quizzical smile. "'Sup, Rockett, what brings you to these parts? Especially since a certain Mr. Rosales is not here today!"

Rockett grimaced. "That's kinda why I stopped off. Is he . . . I mean, do you know why he's absent?"

Wolf's big round eyes widened. "Of all people, Rockett, *you* should know why he's not here. You got him in trouble."

Rockett bristled. "*I* didn't get him in trouble. He did that all by himself. But . . ." She softened. "I thought he was going to get detention, which wouldn't account for him being out of school."

Wolf shook his head. "Dude got a little mouthy with Herrera, so he got temporary suspension. His parents went kinda ballistic."

"Thanks — for the info, that is." Rockett slunk away, feeling worse than ever. *Miko gave me the opportunity to lie about seeing him throw the egg, and I turned it down. Now he's in real trouble — mostly because of him, but partly because of me.*

Her spirits lifted when, after a quick trip to the lunch line, she, Nakili, and Dana formed a little circle at the end of their table and dived into party planning. Nakili had already booked the rec room at the swim club. "It's a big space," she noted, "so the decorating committee — that'd be us — is gonna have to get creative."

On the topic of Rockett's invitations, Nakili was all over the first one, with the hat, until Dana dismissed it. "Easy, cheesy, that one's so obvious. The one with the 'arty-smarty-party' rhyme, that's borderline clever."

Nakili turned to Rockett. "Fine, we'll use that one. Okay, next . . . the list. You got it, Dana?"

Fishing in her backpack, Dana produced it. Rockett and Nakili, heads together, scanned it carefully.

It had most of the names of the kids in their class, including Ginger, Viva, Arrow, Jessie, Darnetta, Wolf, Mavis, Arnold, and even kids they didn't hang with much, like Sharla and Bo. Ruben was on the list, though Rockett knew how furious Dana was with him.

Nakili nodded her approval — until she got to the end of it. That's when she made a face.

There were question marks next to these names: Cleve, Max, and Chaz.

And conspicuous by their absence: Nicole, Stephanie, and Whitney.

Eyeballing Dana, Nakili said, "We've got some discussing amongst ourselves to do."

Rockett noted, "You've got everyone here . . ."

"Except snobby Ones and the misguided boys who worship them," Dana finished, pleased with herself.

Nakili shook her head and scowled. "I'm gonna break it down for you. This party isn't about how we feel about certain someones. It's about Miko, and letting her know who her friends are."

"Exactamundo! I believe this list reflects that." Dana was starting to get just the teensiest bit defensive.

"Not really."

Dana whirled around. This time, Rockett spoke up. "If we honestly want to do that, we have to put Cleve on the list. No?"

Nakili nodded. "She's right. Erase the question mark."

Encouraged, Rockett went on. "And *he'd* probably feel more comfortable if Max came, too. I mean, I'm no fan of his, but in certain situations he can be fun."

"Not to mention, he's a close personal friend of Ruben's!" Dana just had to throw that in.

Rockett ignored her. "And Chaz. No one has anything against him, right? He should be invited. Probably."

Nakili couldn't hide a slight blush. "He's good people. In spite of who he chooses to hang with."

Dana frowned. "Okay. We invite him — but not Stephanie. That girl has a crush on him so big it has its own zip code. And speaking of the me-so-greats, you'll note Whitney and Nicole among the so-left-outs. Let's keep it that way."

Surprisingly, Nakili nixed that idea. "You know what, girlfriends? I'm not gonna play that game. Just leaving out three people — that's the kind of thing The Ones would do. And we are better than that. I say we invite them."

Dana fumed. "Bad plan, N! Mark my words. We do that and it just gives them ammo to turn us down. In the most public, evil way possible."

Nakili folded her arms, determined now. "Put 'em on the list."

Dana scowled. "Why?"

"Because this is about Miko, that's why. And because I say so."

This time, Rockett knew enough to butt out!

Meet me at

Purple Moon®

www.purple-moon.com

Rockett's World

Dana grumbled but caved, not before tossing in, "If it's all right with you, Queen Nakili, I've already asked Arrow's band to perform."

Dana flipped around to face Rockett. "In case you were going to suggest another band, Ruben's grounded. I only put him on the list because I'm sure he won't be allowed to come, let alone entertain. *I* won't miss him!"

In spite of their minor conflicts, the girls made a lot of party progress. By the end of lunch, Nakili's natural megawatt smile was in full effect. "Okay! We have our list, our invites, our rec room, and our music. This train has left the station, peeps."

Rockett, psyched, volunteered, "I can print up the invitations tonight and we can hand them out tomorrow . . . if you guys want."

"Done deal." Dana raised her palm for a "slap me five."

"This weekend, we troll the mall for decorations," Nakili suggested.

Rockett thought for a moment. "Are we giving her a gift, or just the party?"

Nakili considered. "The party's all we can afford. Even with your share, Rockett, we're gonna be tight on funds. I don't think there's much left for a —"

"Wait!" Dana, inspired, interrupted. "What if . . . instead of *buying* her something, we make a huge collage and have everyone sign it? That way, the gift will be totally personal and really express what the party's all about."

"Wow! That's a great idea, Dana!" Rockett's enthusiastic thumbs-up reaction was spontaneous.

In fact, had anyone observed the three girls walking out of the lunchroom together that day, he or she might have noted, *There go three best friends*.

What the trio didn't know was that two people, independent of each other, and coming from different directions, *did* observe them — and had very similar reactions.

Jessie looked disappointed and more than a little jealous.

So did Miko.

Confession Session

I feel like I'm on a roller coaster. Going up: When Mrs. Herrera asked me, in confidence, to tutor Cleve, I thought, *Oh, yuck! How totally fun will this not be.* But that first day, when we started actually talking, and then we went for a smoothie, I realized maybe he's okay. Maybe in a totally opposite way, he's been unfairly labeled, too. So we're, like, clicking, which is pretty unbelievable. If people think we're an item? Well . . . *that's* interesting. But, going down: My so-called friends seem to be doing just fine without me!

When Herrera told me that Miko was going to tutor me, I thought, *Where's the fun? Here comes boring brain-girl.* But man, she's not like that at all! Every time we get together to hit the books, Miko comes up with cool stuff to do afterward. And now, everyone thinks we're hanging out. All right! My rep as a chick magnet lives on!

The nerve of Goodstaff, to pull that stunt on me in homeroom! But I found out a secret about him! A little tidbit he told Max, who cannot keep his mouth shut! So I'm gonna fix Cleve's wagon — only he'll never know it's me! Weee-heee!
Rockett can be such a user sometimes! That is one quality I totally can't stand! When she wants my advice, I'm, like, her best friend. But when something — or someone — more interesting comes along, she leaves me flat.

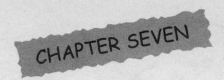

CHAPTER SEVEN

The Miko and Cleve rumor remained headline news at Whistling Pines all day. Teasing the twosome became a game of one-ups.

Just before science class began, Max, still ticked at not being the first to know, chided Cleve. "Dude, you're such a babe magnet, you oughta be teaching physics!"

To which Cleve responded, "It's all about *chemistry*, bro!"

Every time Arnold Zeitbaum walked by Miko, he let out a snort. In Arnold-world, that translated to "Another brainiac abduction!" Every time, Miko just smiled.

Even Sharla Norvell, who pretended to so not care about this stuff, got into it. She stuck magnetic poetry up on Miko's locker that spelled *Cleve and Miko sittin' in a tree, K-I-S-S-I-N-G!*

Miko didn't bother removing it.

The worst moment happened in language arts. That's when Viva passed a note to Miko — only on its journey across the room, it got intercepted by their teacher, Mrs. Tinydahl. She glanced at the outside of the note and said, "Who's 'Mrs. Cleveland Goofstaff'?"

The entire class erupted in hysterics, pointing to Miko.

Amazingly, she didn't even blush!

No one knew how Cleve would have reacted. He wasn't in class that afternoon.

All of which fed the rumor, until it got big and strong. By the end of the day it was approaching *fact* — to everyone but Nicole and her buds.

But a certain member of Her One-ness's loyal clique *had* started to crack. After the girls' room incident — and very much against Nicole's will — Whitney launched a "journalistic investigation." She spent the entire afternoon interviewing sources.

The results? Whitney reported that Miko and Cleve had actually been seen together *outside* school grounds. They'd been spotted sharing a smoothie at the Juice Bar! One day, they shared a couple of slices at Let's Get Some 'Za! An "eyewitness" even placed them in the backseat of Miko's sister's car, "with his arm around her!"

That must have shaken Nicole up. At least Rockett assumed that's what led her to aim a dodgeball at Miko's head in PE. Alas, athletically challenged Nicole sent the ball wide of its target.

Later, after that last-period PE, Rockett was walking to her locker, deep in thought about party decorations. She'd been trying to figure how far up the cheese-o-meter a disco ball would be, when the whispered giggling and clowning around — coming from behind the staircase — compelled her to stop.

"I told you we shouldn't have done that!" *Sounds like . . . Cleve?*

"I totally know. But it was so much fun!" *Could that be . . . Miko?*

Okay, I should keep walking. 'Cause this counts as total eavesdropping. In one minute, I will. . . .

Boy-chuckle. "I know. But tomorrow, we've really gotta buckle down. I could be in deep trouble, Meeks."

Girl-giggles. "You'll be fine, Cleve! I'll totally see to it. But it might not have been too cool for you to miss language arts today. I think people noticed."

Boy-voice: "I had elsewhere to be — you know that."

Girl-sigh: "Okay, we'll just deal. But here's the thing. This weekend? I really need you to do something for me."

"Name it and I'm there. But you gotta promise . . ." He trailed off, because Miko apparently understood.

Next came the sound of backpacks being picked up: a sign that they were about to emerge from their "hiding spot."

Rockett darted away. *Wow! This is a lot more intense than I thought. I need to tell Nakili and Dana, now! Better get to the Birdcage fast!*

Rockett rounded the corner and rushed over to her locker. She'd opened it, about to pull out her homework books, when she felt a tap on the shoulder.

Assuming it was one of the CSGs, she blurted, "You will not be*lieve* what I just overheard!"

Later, Rockett would recall what her father always

said about jumping to conclusions. At that moment, all she felt was foolish when Miko said, *"I'd* like to know what you just overheard. Unless it's on a need-to-know, for-certain-people-only basis."

"Miko!" Rockett's face turned tomato red. She sputtered, "I'm . . . I didn't realize it was you."

"Obviously."

Because Rockett couldn't gauge Miko's mood, she quickly said, "I was going to call you."

"Me too. You, that is."

"Look . . ." they both began. And started to laugh.

"You first," Miko urged.

Rockett drew a sharp breath. *How do I even start to put this?* "Okay. Is everything, you know, all right? You seem kinda, I don't know, different lately."

Miko's eyebrows shot up. "Different? How?"

"W-well," Rockett stammered. She was so not ready to go to the heart of either matter: Cleve, or the Ruben lie! Instead, she ventured, "You haven't been around much lately. I mean, you've been at school and all. But with, you know, not with the CSGs."

Miko considered. "I have been totally busy. . . ."

Rockett opened her mouth to speak, but hesitated. *Should I say that Nakili and Dana think you don't like them anymore? If I do, that could clear everything up, and everyone will be friends again.*

At that instant, it seemed Miko read Rockett's mind. "Anyway, Nakili and Dana aren't exactly lacking for friends. I saw you walking out of the cafeteria with them today. The three of you seemed, I don't know, like you were in your own world, or something."

Rockett was stunned. "So . . . *that's* it? Miko! You *can't* think I'm taking your place with the CSGs or something! That could never —"

"No! I don't think that. I just meant, it's a good thing. Like you said, I've been busy, and this way they don't miss me. Or something — I don't know." Miko sounded convincing . . . not at all.

Rockett let it go. "So anyway, what did you want to ask?"

Miko looked around. The hallway was beginning to fill up with kids crowding around the lockers. She lowered her voice. "There's kind of this thing I've been meaning to talk to you about."

This is it! She's gonna tell me about Cleve! "I'm all ears."

Only just then Nicole and Stephanie brushed by, laughing. Nicole glared in their direction, then tossed back her hair, model-like, and pranced down the corridor. Her friend had to scurry to catch up.

Miko frowned. "This isn't a great place to talk. Can you come over to my house?"

A half hour later, Rockett found herself sitting on Miko's bed, as her friend surveyed herself in the full-length mirror.

Miko's hands were on her hips, and she addressed

Rockett through her reflection. "I've decided to change my look."

"Your look?"

"Actually" — Miko twirled around to face her — "not just my look. My total image."

Rockett squirmed and sat on her hands. "What exactly is your image?"

Crossing her arms, Miko said sarcastically, "Like you don't know? The 'play by the rules, color between the lines, honor roll' girl. Aces every test, little or no studying required. Does that about sum it up?"

Weakly, Rockett replied, "What's wrong with that?"

Miko frowned. "What's *wrong* with that? How do you spell *bo*-ring!"

Rockett protested, "You're not boring! You're unique. You're . . . you." *How majorly lame was that? If someone said that to me, I'd go —*

"You don't understand!" Letting out a huge sigh, Miko flounced on the bed next to Rockett. "I'm determined to do this. I've already started, in case you hadn't noticed."

"Um, I have noticed, Miko. We all have."

"Really?" Miko seemed pleased.

Rockett had so not meant it as a compliment. The black clothes, the trendy platforms — while that look might be okay for someone else, it wasn't Miko.

She tried to be diplomatic. "I'm all for experimenting with different styles and stuff. . . ."

"But . . . ? I know there's a *but* coming."

She's right. There is. Okay, here goes: "Is this about Cleve?"

Miko looked at her funny. "Excuse me?"

I better spill this now. "I have a confession. This is all my fault. The rumor —"

But Miko stopped her. "It's not about Cleve. And as for the rumor, let's just not go there, okay?"

Let's not go there? She's telling me nothing! "But it's almost like you don't mind that people are spreading . . . well, talking about you."

Miko shrugged. "Maybe I don't care what people say."

"Or . . ." Rockett paused. She decided to go straight for it. "Maybe it's true? Everyone knows you two have been spending a lot of time together. And, well, I accidentally heard you under the stairwell."

Miko burst out laughing and slapped the bedcover. "Under the stairwell? You mean, just before dismissal today? So that's what you were going to tell Nakili and Dana you overheard?"

Oops. Busted. Rockett blushed.

Miko caught her breath, then explained, "I'm spending a lot of time with Cleve because Mrs. Herrera asked me to tutor him. His grades are in a free fall."

"Really? That's it? Why haven't you just said so?"

"Cleve asked me not to. And I respect his wishes, that's all."

Rockett considered. "So . . . tutoring? That's it?"

Miko hesitated. Carefully, she added, "Okay, well, it

68

started out as that. But lately, I admit, we've been hanging out a little. You know, as friends."

And I believe that one — right!

Rockett tilted her head. "Come on. You can tell me. Are you sure this whole 'I want a new image' isn't about Cleve? Or boys in general?"

Miko popped up off the bed and pranced around her room, with frequent pauses at the mirror. "Can we leave Cleve for a second? Can't a girl want a different look without it being about boys?"

"Sure, but —"

"Now that you bring it up, okay, I wouldn't *mind* if boys saw me as something more than just smart-girl, you know?"

Rockett was about to protest, but Miko stopped her. "Don't. You know that's how boys see me, because that's how everyone sees me. That's how *I* see me sometimes! So I want a change. And I'm asking for your help."

I can't tell her I don't like her new look. How rude would that be? Warily, Rockett replied, "Help . . . to do what, exactly?"

"I just want to really look — and be — different."

"This isn't exactly my area of expertise," Rockett stalled.

"Yet you have three qualities that will be totally helpful. One: You're artistic and creative. Two: You can keep a secret. I don't want it all over the school why I'm doing this. Let people just learn to accept the new me."

Rockett bit her lip. "What's three?"

"The most important one: You're my friend."

This is bogus! No matter what she says, it's so obvious! Herrera threw her and Cleve together and he's totally rubbed off on her! She's even trying to dress to impress him. Changing yourself to attract boys — that's everything I'm against! I will not help her. But . . . she didn't go to Nakili or Dana. She confided in me. She trusts me. If she only knew what I told Ruben, she probably wouldn't! No matter what, Miko's friendship means a lot to me. So should I do something I don't believe in, just to help a friend?

Confession Session

If I'd gone to Nakili, she would have tried to talk me out of this. And Dana, she'd have totally put me down. But Rockett likes it when people go to her for advice. And I meant what I said — she is a good friend, and she'll put that ahead of her doubts.

So I told Miko one of my biggest secrets today — that I was left back in school one year. And that's why I *have* to get my grades back up. I can't risk *that* again! But I also have to leave school early some days, because Cindy gets out earlier than we do, and I have to see her — and *be* seen with her. High school is where I would have been this year if I hadn't been held back. And Miko was so cool about it — she didn't make fun of me, or think less of me. She's really helping me and being a friend, too.

I am beyond livid!! While I was keeping an eye on Rockett — to make sure she's not spreading any more false rumors — I saw her lurking around by the stairs. So I followed her. And it turned out she was listening to — ugh! — Cleve and Miko behind the staircase! I thought we were so over this. Forget Rockett now, she's not worth my time. But who does Miko think she is?

CHAPTER EIGHT

"I hear you, Miko." Rockett tried to balance total support with total truth. Since they were total opposites, it was tricky.

"Good!" Miko replied, not expecting the rest of Rockett's response.

Which was: "And I so *would* help you. But this . . . this . . . image change thing, you sure it's a good idea? Besides, if it *is* about boys, even a little, I'm probably not the best person to ask. I don't believe in changing the way you look or act for a boy." *Hmmm, that came out sort of harsh. Better soften it.*

She tacked on, "And it's not like I'm some kind of boy magnet, anyway."

What Miko said next stunned Rockett — into submission. Sharply, she pointed out, "Yet you had no trouble attracting the boy you like."

"Huh?"

"Everyone knows you have a crush on Ruben. And it's obvious he likes you back."

Feeling a blush creeping up her neck, Rockett countered, "Untrue. And anyway, no he doesn't."

"Come on, Rockett! He knows we *both* told on him to Herrera. All yesterday afternoon, he shot me daggers. But he's totally friendly with you — I saw the two of you together after school. If he didn't like you, why would he be so quick to forgive you?"

Rockett went pale. She barely managed to squeak out, "How can I help you?"

Miko brightened. "Come to my sister's room. She's got an amazing collection in her closet. Help me try stuff on and see what'll fit my new image. Oh, and I'm totally getting contacts — I am so sick of these glasses! But here's the main thing. I want you to come with me to the Makeup Emporium. I want to try on that new glitter and I need your opinion. You'll come, right?"

"Sure." Rockett's lack of enthusiasm was obvious. Even more so when Miko casually mentioned the rest of her plans.

While they were digging through her sister's closet, Miko slyly said, "You know the science test that's coming up?"

"What about it?"

"Well, maybe I won't do that great on it."

Rockett was aghast. "Miko! No! You can't purposely blow a test!"

She shrugged. "It won't matter what I look like, if I keep acing every test. Then it'll just be the same old me, in a new package."

Rockett suddenly remembered how Dana described Miko spacing on the Shakespeare sonnet in language arts the other day. She folded her arms across her chest. "I said I'd help you, and keep your secret, but if you purposely mess up in class? Color me gone. 'Cause you called me a friend and a real friend would draw the line at that."

For emphasis, she added, "Nakili and Dana sure would!"

Miko threw her hands up defensively. "Whoa! All right, okay, I might rethink that part. Now, which tube top should I wear tomorrow? The black . . ."

Rockett barely heard the rest. *This whole sitch is getting worse. I was just about to do what's right and tell her I wouldn't help her — but here I am, agreeing to something I don't believe in, totally out of guilt! How can I let her keep believing Ruben thinks we both told — when just the opposite is true? And sidebar, what could she see in Cleve that would push her to do this?*

A half hour later, Rockett left, feeling lower than a slug. To lift her spirits and take her mind off the events of the afternoon, she raced through her homework and spent the rest of the night refining the invitations to Miko's surprise party. Then she printed them out, borrowed her mom's calligraphy kit, and addressed the envelopes. Totally focused, she worked furiously.

It was late when she called Nakili.

"Hey, night-bird," Nakili cheerfully answered, "I was just doin' my last lap around the homework pool. What's the bulletin?"

The bulletin? If only I could tell you!

Rockett drew a breath. "Um, I got the invites done."

"How'd they come out?"

Truthfully? They looked amazing. "Pretty awesome. I addressed them, too."

Nakili was instantly psyched. "Then we're good to go! Let's meet early before homeroom and stuff 'em into the lockers of everyone we're inviting. I'll call Dana."

"Nakili, uh, there's something else. . . ."

"Go for it."

It's Miko. She says she's just tutoring Cleve, but I know it's more than that. She's dabbling in glitter makeup, contacts, and tube tops! Yuck! And it gets worse! She's purposely gonna tank on the science test! She expects me to help her. And worst of all, she made me promise not to tell. I can't break that promise, not after what I did to Miko already.

"Rockett? You still there? Or did you launch into outer space?" Nakili started to sound impatient. "It's late, girl, and I still have three chapters of *Julie of the Wolves* to read."

Rockett exhaled, deflated. "It's nothing. I mean, I just want to say, you know, thanks for including me in this. It means a lot."

When Rockett, Nakili, and Dana met before homeroom the next day to stuff the invitations into people's lockers, they figured there'd be no one else around.

Wrong. Two distinct sounds made that obvious.

The first was jarring. Someone slammed a locker shut, really hard.

The other was the sound of . . . crunching pine needles?

76

"Yo, Pine!" Dana dashed ahead of them, just in time to round the corner to the corridor where the eighth-grade lockers were located. "Freeze!" she yelled out. But the mysterious Pine whisked down the hall and out of sight.

Not so quick was early-bird number two. She appeared flustered at the sight of Dana, trailed closely by Nakili and Rockett.

"What worm are you trying to catch, Nicole?" Nakili teased.

"What's it to you?" the One retorted.

Dana chortled. "Oh, look who just popped open a fresh can of venom!"

Spinning on her heel, Nicole stalked away. Was it Rockett's imagination, or Nicole's overdone makeup? Her face was this weird shade of cake-icing red.

Nakili turned to her buds, shrugging. "Let's get to work."

Between the three of them, it only took a few minutes to stuff the invitations through the space at the bottom of the lockers.

They decided to meet up between classes to compare RSVP notes.

Responses from their classmates had been quick — and for the most part, positive. While several people wondered if there was some connection between the rumor and the party — which both "starred" Miko — most were just up for what sounded like a cool time.

77

Rockett, Dana, and Nakili gently reminded each person that it was a surprise, and please not to mention it when Miko might overhear.

In homeroom, the first to say "We'll be there" were Arrow, Viva, and Ginger, who'd also agreed to perform. Ginger had pulled Dana aside. "We've started rehearsals already! I'm kinda nervous — if we're bad, no one at school will let us live it down! — but Arrow's all over it. She might even write a special song for Miko. How amazing would that be!"

Chaz Franklin sidled up to Nakili during first-period art class, to whisper that he was definitely coming. Rockett noticed Nakili blushing.

"Food, drinks, music, games, and girls — I'm there" was how Max Diamond had responded to Rockett. She almost asked him about a special girl — namely Jessie — but decided against it.

As Rockett slid into her seat in math class, Arnold Zeitbaum hovered over her. Using the excuse that Miko might overhear, he leaned in way too close before whispering, "M'lady, I am in receipt of your gracious invitation! I shall guard the secret most diligently, and most certainly attend! You can count on me!"

"That's great, Arnold," Rockett replied, she hoped enthusiastically. "I'm glad you can come."

When Arnold retreated, Jessie, in the next seat, passed her a note. "I got the invitation. You did an amazing job."

Grinning, Rockett leaned over the aisle to whisper,

"You'll be there, right? We could probably use some help decorating the rec room. Up for it?"

To her surprise, Jessie said no — to the last part. "I'm definitely coming to the party, but I don't think I can help setting up."

Rockett had no time to wonder if Jessie's turndown had to do with her feeling left out — the class had begun.

Only not the way anyone expected. Mrs. Kalfus, their math teacher, rapped the pointer on the blackboard, and announced, "Did anyone check his or her horoscope today?"

Whitney raised her hand. "I did."

Their teacher grinned. "Did it happen to mention anything about 'a pop quiz in your near future'?"

Confused, Whitney scrunched her nose. "Uh, no . . ."

Mrs. Kalfus shrugged. "Just another reason not to believe in horoscopes! Put your books away now."

Rockett's stomach churned: Would Miko purposely screw this up?

She turned around to try and read the expression on Miko's face — instead, she made accidental eye contact with Ruben. *He's back in school! Whew! The suspension really was temporary, only a day and a half.*

Ruben returned her half smile. Which made her forget about Miko.

She caught up with him after class, determined to make sure he was okay. "So, a pop quiz! How unfair was that? Were you prepared?"

He grinned. "No, but I think I did okay. It wasn't that hard."

Rockett drew a breath. "Look, I heard about the suspension. I'm totally sorry."

He shrugged. "Hey, not your fault."

"Wolf said your parents really went ballistic."

"Yeah, well, they read me the riot act and grounded me."

She ventured, "Do you think you'll be able to come to Miko's party next week? You got the invitation, right?"

Ruben stretched and yawned. "I could be on parole by then, but I wouldn't make *that* scene, no way!"

Rockett swallowed. "Why? Because . . . of Dana?"

"Nah, me and Big Red are cool. I did the 'I'm so sorry' thing. But I still have to make it up to her by doing something nice. Can't wait to find out what she wants. She hasn't decided yet."

Rockett considered. "So I guess you're still mad at Miko, huh?"

Ruben's eyes narrowed. "Let's put it this way, new girl. Right now, Miko Kajiyama's not on my top ten list of favorite people."

Ruben, you've got it all wrong. She was ready to lie for you. It was me who insisted on telling! But how can I say that? How can I let him stay mad at her — especially now, with the party coming up? I so have to tell him the truth.

"I just wish" — Ruben ran his hands through his floppy hair and turned to go — "she'd find the antidote to her Little Miss Can't Be Wrong disease."

Flushed, Rockett grabbed his elbow. "Ruben, wait, I have something to tell you."

"Not now, *chica*. Gotta scoot to my next class."

"But I —"

"Later, *chica*."

Confession Session

At lunchtime, Rockett was headed for the CSG table, when something caught her eye. The Ones — Nicole, Stephanie, and Whitney — were in deep discussion. That was hardly unusual. What made her stop in her tracks was Nicole waving an open envelope: sticking out was the invitation to Miko's party. As Rockett got closer, she saw Stephanie and Whitney had theirs out, too.

Rockett panicked. *Oh, no! They better put those away! We totally asked everyone to keep this a secret. The whole school's being cool — except them! What if Miko walks by and sees it? What if . . . they do something evil, like Dana said? Like purposely spoil the surprise? Should I go over and say something?*

Determined, Rockett boldly strode in their direction — just in time to hear Nicole sniff, "I'm borderline offended by this invitation."

When Stephanie giggled and said, "I'm surprised they invited us," and then shoved her invite back in her bag. Rockett froze in her tracks, a few feet short of them.

Okay, maybe I'll just listen for a few seconds, and approach only if necessary. She turned to the side, pretending to dig through her backpack so they wouldn't notice her. Kids started crowding in, brushing by Rockett. She had to concentrate to hear what they were saying.

Whitney mused, "It could be . . . on the cusp of fun."

Nicole zoned in on Whitney like a heat-seeking torpedo. "Do you have a plate in your head or something?"

Whitney flinched. "I just meant —"

"Meant *what*? Even if *you* wanted to audit the dork-fest, do you think *I'd* even be seen at a fiesta attended by the likes of Arnold Zitbomb?"

Undeterred, Whitney took another tack. "Speaking of guests, Stephanie, I saw Chaz tell Nakili *he* was going. Incentive for you to show, no?"

Before Stephanie could respond, Nicole inserted herself. "Because why exactly? You're scared he might hang with Nakili Abuto if you're not there? Come *on*!"

Stephanie choked on her iced tea, but Whitney came in for the save. "On that note, Nic, how will *you* really feel if Cleve's there and you're not? You know you want to keep an eye on him!"

Nicole fumed. "As if!"

Then the wheels in her brain started to turn and she backpedaled. "But, now that you mention it, Whit, it *would* be quite the place for me to show everyone, beyond a shadow of a doubt, who Cleve is really interested in. Imagine *Miko* thinking she can compete with me! Mousy-girl's not in a *state* of denial, she's the entire continent."

Stephanie chortled, but Whitney reminded them,

"Miko is the guest of honor, the person everyone's there to celebrate. The spotlight will be on her."

Her voice soaked in faux sweetness, Nicole countered, "Is it my fault if I upstage her? Or, if for some reason . . . don't know *why* . . . she might come down with a bad case of inferiority-itis, when she finds, shall we say, an urgent memo in her locker?"

Whitney scrunched her forehead. "What did you do, Nic?"

But Nicole remained enigmatic, adding only, "Besides, it's a surprise party. Hence, Miko doesn't know about it, won't be dressed or made-up — she'll be the most pathetic-looking person at her own shebang."

Whitney glanced over her shoulder. "Sure about that? Look."

Rockett spun around — so did Nicole and Stephanie. Just in time to see Miko headed her way.

Rockett's jaw dropped. That her friend was in makeup overload and clad in a tube top, trendy cargo pants, and squishy platform sandals, wasn't the most shocking part. It was her hair — Miko had done it up in random top-knots. Now, bushy little tails sprouted like crabgrass all over her head.

Did Miko come to school looking like this? We all would have noticed, I'm sure!

Rockett charged into action, heading off Miko before she could get too close to The Ones' table.

"Hey, Miko! You look . . . uh . . . were you wearing this in homeroom? Or art, or math?"

Miko giggled. "No, I wasn't sure my parents would let me out of the house like this. So I changed just before lunch." She patted her head. "What do you think? I copied this look out of a magazine."

Before Rockett could gather her thoughts to respond, Nicole yelled loud enough for the immediate world to hear, "Hey, Miko, what do you call that 'do? Riot-grrl wanna-be? Or Hair-tastrophe?" She slapped the table for emphasis, cueing Stephanie to howl along with her and all eyes in the cafeteria to turn to Miko. Several people pointed and giggled.

Miko shriveled. More than anything, Rockett wished she could think of a clever, biting comeback on Miko's behalf. But she couldn't.

Cleve could.

Like a hero Prince Charming, he swooped down upon the scene, threw a protective arm around Miko, and casually said, "*I* think she looks cute like this."

Gently, he led her away from The Ones' table and out the door.

Though Rockett spent the rest of the lunch period going over the RSVPs with Nakili and Dana and firming up their plans to go to the mall on Saturday, she was majorly distracted. She was still upset over her exchange with Ruben — not telling him the truth was gnawing at her — and bugged about the bizarro-scene between Miko, The Ones, and Cleve!

That the CSGs weren't upset made it worse.

Nakili believed that Miko would totally come to her senses — about everything — as soon as the party began. To that end, she redoubled her efforts to make sure everything went mega-smoothly.

What Dana believed, Rockett couldn't know. Even as they worked together for the same purpose, they weren't exactly bonding sisters.

Rockett's next class was science, but her head was still in Miko-land. It wasn't until she took her seat that she realized she'd left her textbook in her locker. Mr. Schluss, their teacher, glanced at his wristwatch. "You have exactly three minutes to retrieve it and get back here."

Which would have been plenty of time, had she not found Miko, all alone at the lockers. Sobbing softly.

Alarmed, Rockett raced over. "Miko, what's wrong?"

Shaken, Miko looked up. Her dark eyeliner streaked her cheeks.

I bet it's because Nicole made fun of her hairdo! I can't believe we actually let Nakili bully us into inviting that witch to Miko's party! I'm going to find a way to uninvite her!

Miko continued to whimper quietly. Rockett reached into her knapsack for a tissue. "It's okay. You can tell me anything. Or not, I'll understand. But let's go to the girls' room and do some repair, okay?"

Miko nodded and followed Rockett into the bathroom. It was there that Rockett noticed Miko gripping something in her left hand. It looked like a bunch of torn-out magazine articles. Someone had written all over the top one, but because it was stained with Miko's tears, it was hard to see what it was.

Noticing Rockett trying to eyeball it, Miko softly said, "When I went to get a book, I found this in the bottom of my locker."

Until she read all of it, Rockett was surprised at Miko's hyperreaction. It was just a few of those teen magazine quizzes. The title of the first one was "The Top Ten Reasons Girls Don't Get Boyfriends." The next was "'L' Is for Loser: How to Tell if He's Using You." The third, about extreme fashion faux-pas, was called "Would You Leave the House Looking Like This?" In each case, all the most obvious wrong answers were marked off.

It ended with "Memo to Miko, in case you don't get the message: Boys aren't like those awards you swipe so easily — they have to like you back. PS: The one you *think* likes you, *doesn't*! And PPS: Even your so-called best friends won't tell you, so consider this a favor. I don't know what you're trying to prove, but you look hideous. Signed: SomeOne who knows.

Suddenly, Rockett remembered hearing the slamming of a locker early in the morning, and Nicole's "busted" expression. She fumed. "That does it! I'm so going to get Nicole for this! How'd she even get into your locker, anyway?"

Finally, wiping away her tears, Miko said, "Forget it. It's . . . okay."

"Not! She's treating you like dirt! Maybe you can let her, but I can't!"

88

Miko sniffed, and a half smile formed on her lips. "It's ironic in a silly way. All the years we've gone to school together, Nicole never paid any attention to me. It's like I was invisible to her and The Ones. And now she's spending all this time trying to make me feel bad."

Rockett thought for a moment. "Nicole is majorly jealous — I haven't seen her act like this ever. But it was kinda cool the way Cleve popped up like that."

"What's so weird is that Nicole thinks this is all about Cleve. It isn't. . . ."

As gently as she could, Rockett said, "If it's not about Cleve, then why would those stupid articles wig you out so much?"

"I don't know. I tried something totally new today. You know, with my hair? And when it comes to looks and all, I'm not the most confident person in the world. Cleve's helping, I mean, he's being really supportive. But Nicole ranking on me like that and then putting these 'loser' articles in my locker, I don't know, it sort of all hit me at once."

"Don't let her get to you, Miko. She is so not worth it."

"Rockett? Can I tell you something else? In total confidence? Sometimes I'm afraid people don't like me because —"

Rockett refused to let her finish. "*Everyone* likes you, Miko!" *Just hang in until next Saturday, and we'll prove it!*

Miko sighed. "So anyway, remember I asked you to come to the Makeup Emporium with me? There's one in the mall. Are you free on Saturday?"

Rockett's stomach sank. "Oh, Miko, I'm sorry. I can't. I have other plans."

Miko's face, which had brightened for a second, now clouded again. "With Nakili and Dana? Plans that I'm not included in, I guess. Forget it, it's fine. I just changed my mind anyway."

"No, but wait, maybe . . ."

Now she thinks we're purposely leaving her out! I can't tell her the truth, it'll spoil the whole party — we need it more than ever now. But how can I let her down at a time like this? She'll think Cleve is her only friend — which it's starting to look like! I guess I could tell Nakili and Dana that I'm not going with them . . . but we're all set to do this together. And, okay, selfish-reason alert, I really want to do this with them. This is the fun part!!

Confession Session

No way is Nicole gonna trip out Miko. I mean, I don't want to lose Nic — it's very, very good to be seen with her. But what can a guy do? So many girls, so little time! Speaking of which, the Pine seems to know more than he should about my social life. He left this note in my locker: "*I know the game you're playing. About those unexplained absences, and about a certain girl.*" Whatever the Pine knows, he better be keeping it under his needles, or he might get stung!

At first,
Nicole's swipes
didn't get to me. It
was really kind of funny
that she's jealous — over
Cleve, no less! But today, she got
me. I wasn't sure how the hair
thing would really look. When
she made fun of me in front of
the entire cafeteria, I thought I'd
die. And now, these notes in my
locker! I'm trying to act really
cool and confident with this new
look, but inside I'm getting
scared. Maybe I do look kind of
lame. But Nicole's stabs don't
hurt nearly as much as Nakili
and Dana leaving me out. It
looks like Rockett's
their new CSG
sister.

This party has *got* to work. Every day Miko seems to be heading further from us and from our friendship. And that can't happen. I will fix it!

CHAPTER TEN

Though Saturday dawned drizzly and misty, by early afternoon the day had turned bright and crisp. A cool, invigorating breeze filtered through the pine trees.

The weather matched Nakili's mood. She leaned over from the passenger seat to the horn of her dad's car and, as they pulled up in Rockett's driveway, stuck her head out the window, yelling, "Yo, Rockett, got benjamins in your pocket? We're off to the mall, so come on, y'all!"

Her upbeat mood was catching. With a smile a mile wide, Rockett loped out, and after greeting Mr. Abuto, turned to Nakili. "Easy cheesy. Your rhymes are so not flyin', they're dyin' on the vine."

Nakili clapped, threw her head back, and laughed. "So my strong suit might not be poetry. Just watch me with a list! I *rock!*"

With that, she dug into her tote and produced a notebook containing their decorating to-gets, and began reading it off. "We hit Party Palooza for plastic bowls, paper plates, napkins, cups, crepe paper, tape, balloons, disco ball, and glitter. Then, we get art supplies for the collage —"

"Aren't you forgetting something?" Rockett interrupted, noticing the route Mr. Abuto was taking.

"What'd I leave out?" Nakili sounded defensive.

"Uh . . . Dana?"

Nakili's head jerked up from her list, and she yelped, "Pops! Make a left here!"

Dana was waiting outside. Dressed in khaki bell-bottoms with a shirt tied at the waist, she looked breezy as the day. Once inside the car, she arched her eyebrows. "Were we about to forget me?"

Together, Nakili and Rockett exclaimed, "As if!"

Mr. Abuto dropped the girls at the mall's main entrance. "I'll be back to pick you up at five P.M.," he reminded them. "Be outside."

Party Palooza, their first stop, was at the other end of the mall, so the girls headed in that direction. Passing trendy boutiques made Rockett think of Miko. Passing the record store You Got the Music in You brought Ruben to mind.

Dana's mind, that is. "Wonder if detention-boy is planning to show up? He's one of the few AWOLs on our RSVP list."

Nakili, swinging her large straw tote, noted, "Would he even want to come? He's not exactly down with a 'Miko's all that' bash."

Lightbulb! Rockett stopped in her tracks and grabbed Dana's elbow. "About that, Dana . . ."

Dana swung around and arched her eyebrows. "*Sí, señorita . . . ?*"

"I talked to Ruben, and he, uh, mentioned, that — as

part of his penance — he has to do something nice for you."

She grinned mischievously. "I'm still deciding on that one. I was thinking of scut work, like making him mow my lawn, or typing my report. . . ."

Rockett went for it. "I have another idea. 'Cause Nakili nailed it, Ruben *doesn't* want to come to the party. So for that personal favor to you, could you, maybe, ask him to forgive Miko and come to the party?"

They resumed walking, and Dana shook her head. "You are something else, Rockett-girl! Anything to be with crush-boy. You must be desperate, to ask *me!*"

Rockett bristled. "If that's what you need to believe, Dana, go for it. But, as you know, *any* party is more fun with Ruben there. More important, *this* party is for Miko. It's to show her who her real friends are — and how much better will she feel if Ruben comes? That would prove he's not mad at her anymore."

Nakili was with it. "She's on the logic train, D."

Amused, Dana curled her hair around her forefinger. "How selfless! Rockett, of course, has nothing to gain by his presence. Well, maybe I'll ask him, maybe not. I'll see . . . if I feel like it."

Nakili spun around and got in Dana's face. "Feel like it, okay?"

Party Palooza lived up to its name. The place was a bodacious bazaar of paper goods. Once inside, Rockett had a major brainstorm. "Since Miko won the chess tournament, why not use chess as our decorating theme? We could construct giant cardboard chess pieces and place them around the room."

"We could insert pictures of Miko's face inside each one!" Nakili added.

Dana agreed. "And maybe we'll make a banner to hang across the back wall or something that says, 'Queen Miko Rules!'"

Inspired, the girls got busy stocking up on crepe paper, streamers, balloons, and other decorating doodads. An hour later, they emerged, happily laden with huge, brightly colored Party Palooza shopping bags.

"That was phat!" Nakili said. "We are rolling! Now we need to get oak tag, markers, glue, and tape for the giant chess pieces. We also need stuff for the collage. That store's upstairs. Looks like the nearest escalator is over there." She pointed to the right.

"Cool, that'll still give us plenty of time for a food court break before we shop some more," Dana noted. "I wouldn't mind checking out a new top."

Dana had just put one foot on the escalator's first step — the exact second that Rockett, glancing up, saw them. At the top of the "down" escalator, poised to get on, were two way familiar faces.

Miko. And Cleve.

Rockett panicked. *They cannot see us! We've got these Party Palooza shopping bags! They'll know! We can't go up now!*

But it was too late. Not only was Dana on her way up, so was Nakili. Acting on sheer, if misguided impulse, Rockett yanked on the back of Dana's shirt. Only since it was tied at the waist, all that did was make it untie. Domino effect: Dana went apoplectic. Furious, she whirled around.

Unfortunately, at that nanosecond, Rockett was faring even less gracefully with Nakili. She'd grabbed her by the straw bag — which made the unzipped tote go flying. Which, dominolike again, caused all of Nakili's stuff to pop out and sail over the escalator to the floor!

The girls screamed and ran down the up escalator to pick up the stuff.

Dana shrieked, "What is wrong with you, Rockett?"

Nakili, bewildered and frantically trying to retrieve her stuff, was all, "What the dilly, yo?"

Rockett tried desperately to use facial motions — and not point — to explain her actions. It worked: Dana and Nakili realized they'd almost bumped into Cleve and Miko. Miraculously, Cleve and Miko didn't hear the clumsy commotion below. A toddler darted in front of them and they had to take a step back to allow the child's frantic mom to catch him.

Now Nakili said, "C'mon, girlfriends, they're coming down. Hide!"

There was a freestanding cart selling jewelry right by the bottom of the escalator: The girls quickly crouched behind it.

Dana, still retying her shirt, was far, far from amused.

She seethed, "You made us look like the pratfall posse."

From their hiding spot, the trio watched the frolicsome twosome, side by side on the "down" escalator.

Dana emitted a yelp. "He's squeezing her shoulder! Everyone who thinks *ick*, raise your hand!"

Nakili shook her head. "Even after what you've been saying . . . what everyone's been saying, and what I saw in the cafeteria yesterday, I still didn't want to believe this. But now . . ."

If I'd agreed to go with her, Miko probably wouldn't be here with him! I feel so bad, but at least she didn't see us. She'd know we had these plans and didn't include her. The least I can do for Miko is try to play the Cleve crush down — even though I don't believe her, she is denying it.

"Uh, maybe it's not exactly what it looks like."

Dana was all over her. "Knock, knock, was it not *you* who exposed this strange little romance in the first place? Much as it pains me to admit, you were right. So *now* is when you backpedal? You really are too much."

Rockett swallowed. *I know I wasn't supposed to tell, but . . .*

"Look, you guys, promise you won't say anything, because Cleve is like, embarrassed or something. Principal Herrera asked Miko to tutor Cleve. That's one big reason why they've been spending so much time together. . . ." She trailed off, because *that* surely didn't explain *this*.

And Dana believed *that* . . . not for a second. "Just

study-buddies, huh? Stop cracking my taco, Rockett. They're obviously a lot more."

Nakili added, "Look at the shopping bags she's got. They're all from designer and accessory boutiques. Not even a bookstore in the mix."

Devilishly, Dana went, "Of course, there is one way to find out what's up. We could follow them — see what develops."

"No!" Rockett protested. "What if they discover us? With these shopping bags? We'll have blown our own surprise."

Nakili made the decision. "We'll tail 'em for a little while. Just to see if we find out anything else. Then we'll finish up what we came for."

As unobtrusively as possible, trying not to rustle their own shopping bags, the girls trailed Miko and Cleve. They stayed as far behind as they could, while still keeping them in sight. Rockett had a sinking feeling about where they were headed. . . .

"The Makeup Emporium?" Nakili was puzzled.

Because she felt like an outlaw sneaking after Miko and Cleve, an unexpected tap on her shoulder made Rockett gasp and jump sky-high. She spun around, only to come face-to-face with . . . Whitney and Stephanie.

Rockett was speechless.

Dana wasn't. "Spying on behalf of your great leader? Where is Nasty Nic, anyway?"

Annoyed, Stephanie retorted, "She's not our leader,

she's our friend. She planned to be here but couldn't make it."

"Why, did she break a nail?" Dana goaded.

But Whitney and Stephanie were more into watching Cleve and Miko than sparring with the CSGs. "Why would Miko take Cleve shopping for her makeup?" Whitney wondered. "You do that with your girlfriends, not with a guy."

"Maybe," Stephanie said pointedly, "she *has* no girl-friends to do this with."

Nakili didn't usually have a temper. But when she did, ducking was an excellent option. She laced into Stephanie, seething, "This is an A and B gathering, girl, so why don't you just C your way out of it!"

It worked. Whitney and Stephanie turned and slinked away.

When they were out of earshot, Dana applauded. "Good one, didn't know you had it in you. Still want them invited?"

Nakili frowned, but didn't answer. While eyeballing Miko, who was in the body glitter section, she finally said, "Enough with this. We came to accomplish something. Let's just do it, and leave the stupid spy tactics to the jelly-brained double-oh-sevens."

That, as it turned out, was easier said than done. For now that they were consciously trying to avoid Miko and Cleve, they seemed to almost bump into them every-where they went. As they left Color Me Mine, Miko and

Cleve rounded the corner. They darted into the Bon-Bon Boutique, just missing them, and then had to practically play hide-and-seek in Books 'n More to keep from being discovered.

Worse, they couldn't avoid Whitney and Stephanie, who'd resumed tailing the twosome. Could it be more obvious that they planned to report everything to Nicole?

Amazingly, Cleve and Miko never seemed to notice they were being spied on by The Ones, or being purposely avoided by the CSGs. The duo made their way from the Makeup Emporium to Shoe-Biz, to Necessary Accessories, to Be a Sport.

Every time Rockett saw them, she felt worse and worse that she'd turned Miko down. At the food court, where they'd finally taken a break, Rockett was too distracted to eat, and pushed her food around on the plate.

Which Nakili picked up on. "Don't be bummed. Nothin's not fixable. Not in Nakili-land anyway."

Rockett spilled . . . some of it. "You don't understand. When I spent the afternoon at Miko's yesterday? She asked me to come to the mall with her today. Because we were doing this, I turned her down. She seemed really upset."

Nakili pressed her fingers to her forehead. "Idea."

"For . . . what?" Rockett asked.

"For the one thing we haven't figured out yet. Namely: How we get Ms. Miko to her own par-tay."

Dana rolled her eyes but urged, "Tell us, oh wise one."

"It's obvious Miko wants to be doin' stuff with us — even if she can't come out and say it to anyone but Rockett."

"Who's not technically a CSG." Dana *had* to add that. Rockett began to think of it as a reflex, something Dana had no control over!

Nakili ignored her. "So here's a plan. How 'bout if Rockett invites her to the movies on Saturday night, and then, on the way, just makes a detour to the swim club, and then to the rec room?"

"Under what pretext?" Rockett asked, unsure.

"Make something up. Tell her you need to check it out. Maybe your little brother left a video game there and you said you'd get it."

Rockett considered. "That could work, but she'll hardly be dressed for a party if she thinks we're going to the movies."

"Not a problem," Dana pointed out, just as Miko and Cleve ambled by — swinging shopping bags with designer logos. "She's turned into a twenty-four-seven fashionista. One can only wonder what she'd wear to the movies!"

Suddenly, Miko turned. She stared straight at them. It would have been better if she'd said something . . . anything. But she didn't. She slipped her arm in Cleve's and made a sharp U-ie. Had she noticed their shopping bags from Party Palooza? Or was she too focused on the three of them together, without her?

Nakili swallowed hard. "One more week. Then this

will all be behind us. We'll get back to where we once belonged."

For once, Dana didn't have a comeback. Later, when Mr. Abuto was driving them home, she said to Rockett, "Hey, look, I've thought it over. I will ask Ruben."

I guess that hurt look in Miko's eyes really knocked the chip off Dana's shoulder.

"Thanks, Dana. I —"

"Say nothing, Rockett. Your silence is all the thanks I need."

While Dana and Nakili were going to work on constructing the giant cardboard chess pieces, Rockett had taken the supplies for the collage home. Her mom was a collage artist, and Rockett was planning to hit her up for ideas. Which her mom was more than happy to supply. In fact, it was Mrs. Movado who came up with the idea to design the collage like a giant chessboard, and give each of Miko's friends one box for a personal expression.

After dinner Rockett decided to catch up on her e-mails. There were more than she expected. A cute forward from her sister, Juno, called "Life Lessons." A chatty one from her best friend Meg; an RVSP to the party from Mavis, who chose to add, "Remember, Rockett, what I have been saying from the start. This rumor you have started does not have a basis in truisms." And a really cute poem from Sharla.

Rockett responded to each one. She was just about to shut down the computer, when one more came on the screen. At first, Rockett didn't recognize the address: Who was WPMT? It wasn't until she saw the signature that she realized it stood for "Whistling Pines Mystery Tree."

The message sent her reeling.

"Rockett! I have some secret 411 4-U. Cleve Good-staff is in trouble! Not only because of his grades. He was caught cutting classes! Mrs. Herrera suspects he has forged excuses, but doesn't know for sure yet. There is more! He cut to see his girlfriend, Cindy, who goes to high school and gets out earlier than he does. He has left early on several occasions to meet her. I thought you, Rockett, should know this. — the Pine"

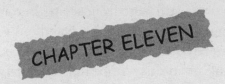

CHAPTER ELEVEN

"Is Miko home?" Rockett was pretty sure it was Miko's sister, Saki, who'd answered the phone. She wasn't sure exactly what to say when Miko got on the line.

"She's out shopping," Saki answered. "Who's this?"

"Her friend Rockett. Do you know when she'll be back?"

"I'm not sure."

Still? Wow. "Would you tell her to call me when she gets home?"

Rockett had been all set to tell Miko about the incriminating e-mail she just got — but between the time she made the call and the next day when Miko returned it, she flip-flopped. Nakili's firm belief, *"One more week. Then this will all be behind us . . ."* stopped her.

Nakili *had* to be right. Miko has to get over Cleve — as soon as possible! And the party will do it. It will totally make Miko see how many *real* friends she has. People who like her just the way she is — was, that is. Or something. After that, finding out about Cleve and his high-school girlfriend, and the real reason he was in trouble, won't hurt her as much. It'll soften the blow at least.

So when Miko did call back, Rockett simply asked her to come to the movies on Saturday. As planned.

Miko was wary, still hurt from seeing her at the mall. "Sure you wouldn't rather be with Nakili and Dana?"

Rockett tried to be casual. "Come on, Miko. It's so not what you think. And this will be fun. The scary new flick at the multiplex is supposed to be incredible. We'll have a kickin' time."

Finally, Miko agreed. And Rockett breathed a major sigh of relief.

Fortunately, the week before the party wasn't nearly as drama-drenched as the preceding one had been. Now that the shock waves set off by the rumor had subsided, the entire school settled down and got back to normal. Correction: normal times the speed of light! Rockett couldn't remember ever being so busy.

Their teachers must have had party-radar. To a one, they did their best to complicate matters by piling on the work. And because Rockett had promised to help Miko refine her new image, she went shopping for new clothes and accessories with her on a couple of afternoons.

In addition, she, Nakili, and Dana were furiously focused on the party. Each day after school, post soccer practice, yearbook meetings, or extra-credit art assignments, they met at the rec room to decorate. By midweek, with lots of help from their families, the crepe paper was up, as was the disco ball and the hanging paper moons, stars, suns, and streamers. When they added the cardboard cutout chess pieces and balloon bouquets, it would really look ragin'.

*   *   *

While Dana and Nakili were on food and drink patrol, Rockett's job was to put the finishing touches on Miko's magnificent gift: the collage. It was huge, four poster boards stuck together. The idea to design it as a giant chessboard totally rocked. Inside each square was room for Miko's friends to add a personal memory, or a memento, of a meaningful moment spent with her. Or even a cool note of congrats would fit in just as well.

The response was mega! On Thursday, Rockett's spirits soared as each person came to the library, where she'd hid the collage, to add his or her personal bit.

Rockett put hers in first. It was a campaign poster, a reminder of when she, Miko, and Nakili came "this close" to winning the class elections. Nakili elected to paste a picture of herself, Dana, and Miko from third grade in their Three Musketeers Halloween costumes. It was a subtle reminder of the CSG sisterhood. Dana had also added a group picture. Under it she penned, *"All I can remember is the three of us together, always."*

Jessie and Darnetta came in and greeted Rockett as if there'd been no tension at all. They used two boxes to pen an "ode to friendship." Jessie wrote, "Some people make the world more special just by being in it. Miko, this means you!!" Darnetta had added, "Friendship is a great place. I'm glad we're there."

It surprised no one that Mavis's contribution was "You are a nice person who has many friends. I predict you will stop trying to be someone you're not!" She added, "This will be valuable one day! The signature of a famous seer!"

The boys, of course, had their own — okay, weird — ways of contributing. Arnold's was typically bizarre. "On behalf of the Knights of the Purple Orchid, I salute thee, fair maiden Miko, on thy honorable accomplishments! May the Force be with you!"

Max stuck a dollar bill onto the collage and signed it! Rockett didn't even want to try and figure out the significance of that!

Wolf DuBois taped up a menu from his parents restaurant, a reminder of a giggle-filled lunch they once had there. Bo Pezanski just signed his name.

Rockett wasn't sure what The Ones would do. They'd said they were coming to the party, but it didn't mean they'd contribute to the gift. She wasn't sure she even *wanted* them to — not after seeing them at the mall.

When Whitney walked into the library, Rockett didn't try to hide her suspicions. "You're going to do something *nice* on this collage, right?"

Whitney smiled and winked as she fished a marker out of her slingback bag. With her customary flourish, in huge letters, she wrote, "Congratulations, Miko," putting little hearts on top of the *i*'s.

On her heels, Stephanie flounced in, clutching a delicate and colorful dried flower arrangement.

"Those are amazing." Rockett gave her props.

"Well, chuh! They're from me," Steph responded,

then softened. "These are from a camping trip Miko and I were on."

Rockett was afraid to ponder what Nicole's contribution would be — or if she'd even bother. But halfway into the period, Nicole sashayed in, sniffling, "I heard there was something for me to sign."

Before Rockett could respond, Nicole whipped out a feather-tipped pink marker and — taking the spot right in the middle — wrote, "Congratulations, little Miko! On . . . whatever! Love, Nicole & Cleve."

Rockett was stunned. *So, there's a little secret named Cindy that Nicole doesn't know about — how I'd love to tell her! But writing this on the collage just stinks. She'll do anything to make Miko feel bad.*

Steaming, she got right in Nicole's face. "How could you do this?"

Nicole feigned surprise. "What do you mean? Cleve's my date for the cute little kudo-fest you're throwing, so naturally, I signed the gift from both of us."

Rockett couldn't hide a small smirk. "Cleve's your . . . date, huh? Does *he* know?"

Nicole rolled her eyes and turned to leave. "Bored now."

Rockett wondered if she could try to erase it, but just then, Arrow, Viva, and Ginger walked in to add their mementos.

Arrow had pasted movie stubs; Viva, a concert program; Ginger actually got hold of Miko's very first soccer jersey — in a child size 6! — and tacked it on the collage, with a note: "Goal-friends now, Girl-friends forever!"

And Rockett suddenly saw in Ginger what Dana obviously got. She was a girl with a really good heart.

But Rockett was most touched by Sharla's attempt at a haiku poem, an homage to Miko's win in that contest.

By the end of the day, only Ruben — and Cleve, if you didn't count Nicole's signature — hadn't added anything.

About Cleve, there was nothing Rockett could do. Not so the former. Besides asking if he was coming to the party, Rockett had some unfinished business with Ruben.

She found him in the Birdcage at the end of the day, about to head out to the bus line. It was easy to gauge his mood — clearly, the cloud had lifted. His old sparkle was back. And just like that, Rockett couldn't bring herself to tell him the truth about who really tattled on him that day.

In fact, Ruben greeted her first. "Hey, new girl! What's the good word?"

"I'm hoping there is one. And it's that you're coming to Miko's party."

Ruben laughed. "You gotta worship the grapevine. I guess you heard. For some strange reason, Dana said we'd be five-by-five if I showed. The 'rents were cool with it — so I guess I'll be there."

"I'm really glad, Ruben." *You have no idea how much!*

Confession Session

When Dana told me what the "nice thing" I had to do was, I never expected this! At first I was, no way, man! Miko turned me in, and things have not been easy on the home front because of it. But I guess going to a party beats other stuff she could have asked — like mowing her lawn or something. I don't even have to talk to Miko if I don't feel like it. I wouldn't mind the chance to jam with Arrow and her band, though.

CHAPTER TWELVE

"Rockett, your room looks like Rome after the fall!" Rockett's father had ducked in to assure her that he would drive her to the party. But one glance around, and he got sidetracked. Understandably. Piles of clothes, shoes, hair bands, and jewelry covered the floor.

Rockett had tried on dozens of outfits for the party. Nothing seemed right. She'd hung none of them back up. Now she was trying a powder-blue cap-sleeved dress with ribbon trim, and blue satin platform wedge shoes.

Acknowledging the mess on the floor, she said, "My bad, Dad, I'll clean."

"When?"

She checked her watch and shook her head. "Not tonight. I told Miko we'd pick her up in, like, twenty minutes." Rockett regarded herself in the mirror. The dress was sorta happening, but she wasn't sure about the shoes. Against her better judgment she asked for an opinion. "What do you think, Dad?"

"I think you look beautiful, sweetheart."

Rockett ripped off the entire outfit. Ten minutes later, she'd settled on a purple three-quarter-sleeve T-shirt, gray skirt, bump-toe platform Mary Janes, and a star necklace.

As she bolted out the door, it occurred to her she had no clue what Miko would look like. . . .

"Wow! Miko, you look . . . really . . . uh . . . this totally goes with your new image!" That was the best Rockett could manage, when, promptly at seven-thirty, she rang her friend's doorbell and Miko answered it. Rockett was so nervous, she was sure Miko could hear the sound of butterflies flapping in her stomach.

Miko didn't look horrendous. Exactly. Her short-sleeved blue dress was kinda similar to the one Rockett almost wore. What screamed were the accessories: She was on jewelry overload. It wasn't just the red-and-silver beaded choker. Or the triple-bangled matching bracelet. Or even the butterfly earrings — though you could make a case for "yuck" on those alone. No, Rockett thought as she and Miko slipped into the backseat of her dad's car, it was that red-and-silver beaded thing on her head, capped off by the huge clip that was holding back . . . uh . . . half her hair.

"What do you think of the glitter body art?" Miko was asking, pointing out her shimmering arms and neck. Rockett hadn't even noticed that!

"It's . . . uh . . . it works. Totally," Rockett fibbed. *This is how she's dressed for the movies? Maybe she knows! Maybe Cleve tipped her off — or worse, Nicole!*

But then Miko said, "I know what you're thinking. *Isn't she kind of overdone for the movies?* But after what happened in school the other day, I figured it's better to try this stuff out when I'm just with one good friend — not in front of everyone at once."

Going down? Rockett's stomach plunged like a water balloon dropped off a rooftop. She barely squeaked out a smile.

"So, anyway, what did you say the name of this movie was?" Miko asked.

For a split second, Rockett spaced. Luckily, her dad didn't. Swinging around from the driver's seat, he prompted, "Isn't it *Horror Junior High*, or something like that?"

"Yes!" Rockett yelled, a little too loudly.

Her dad waited until he pulled out of the driveway and made a left down Miko's street, before reciting the lines he and Rockett had rehearsed. "The movie doesn't start until eight, would you mind if I swung by the swim club for a minute? I think Jasper left his video game there. In the rec room."

Miko shrugged nonchalantly. Which made Rockett pretty secure that the guest of honor didn't suspect anything.

Still, Rockett was sweating by the time they pulled up. *Please, everyone, be there by now! If someone's being dropped off, it'll blow it! We've made it this far!*

Meanwhile, her dad dutifully kept to the "script." "Rockett, sweetheart, would you mind going in and looking around? That way I don't have to find a parking spot."

"Sure, Dad."

"And hey," he said, snapping his fingers as if he'd just thought of it. "If Miko goes with you, you might find Jasper's lost video game faster. How 'bout it, you two?"

With each step nearer the door, Rockett's heart thumped louder. How could Miko not hear it? Or the whispering she was sure she heard coming from inside? You'd think those guys could seriously zip it — for another few seconds at least! The party-goers knew she and Miko were approaching — Rockett's dad had done a quick car-phone call to the rec room to alert them.

Please, please, let this be a real . . .

"SURPRISE!"

Rockett thought her seismic sigh of relief might be louder than the sound-barrier-shattering shouts of "Surprise! Surprise!" that joyously blasted them through the door.

Not close. For as the lights were thrown on, the rec room, which had seemed cavernous when they first rented it, was now filled to capacity and decorated to the max. The garrulous greeting was accompanied by Arrow and the Explorers doing a kicking version of "Celebrate," timed perfectly to accompany Miko's entrance. The moment was beyond amazing — magical, really!

At first, it seemed everyone was there — all the kids from school, plus all the CSG families and friends. The crowd rushed Miko as one, and in a flash, she was swallowed up in a whoosh of well-wishers.

Rockett took a second to deal with the decorations.

Balloon arches, bursting with color, stretched from one end of the room to the other. The cardboard cutout chess pieces, placed randomly around the room, were totally inspired. So were the flowers, dangling suns, moons, and stars — the disco ball . . . well, okay, it was cheesy, but it worked.

Best of all was the banner: CONGRATULATIONS, MIKO! U R OUR CHAMP!

In the crowd, she saw Nakili, who'd gone with a flower-patterned dress, while Dana had chosen a cool vest over a button-down shirt. Nicole's fashion statement was to curl her usually stick-straight hair. The perm worked — she practically screamed "special occasion." That girl really did have effortless style. Of course, that hardly compared to Stephanie, who wore a sparkly tiara in her hair! Whitney looked bubbly, and even Mavis had made an effort, by wearing a dress. In her world, that was a total nod to the event.

Rockett caught glimpses of Wolf, and Bo and Sharla, Jessie and Darnetta, all part of the crowd trying to get close to Miko.

Rockett's eye roamed the room for Ruben. She found him on the fringes of the crowd, wearing cargo pants and a T-shirt, playing air guitar. *I hope he jams with Arrow! That would be beyond cool.*

So swept up in the moment was Rockett that she nearly didn't notice. But after a few minutes, Miko extracted herself from the crowd. She summoned Nakili,

Dana, and Rockett and motioned that she wanted to talk to them.

In private.

Massive! Miko is so blown away by the surprise party, she can't wait to tell us how much she appreciates this!

Or not.

Miko shuttled her friends into the empty coat room, and closed the door. She checked around to make sure they were alone.

And then . . . she *exploded!*

"This is the worst thing you could have done!" Miko was practically seething.

Dana looked nervous. Her attempt at a quip fell flat. "Maybe it's just me, but does anyone else get the feeling that Miko . . . isn't, uh . . . cheered by this celebration?"

Shaken, Nakili gulped. "What's wrong? We thought you'd be psyched."

Miko threw her hands on her hips. "Really? Have you even been noticing me these past few weeks? Or have I become totally invisible to you?"

Rockett jumped in. "Wait a sec, Miko, that's unfair. You're pretty much all we've been thinking about."

"Or did you think this party spontaneously erupted?" Dana asked.

Nakili added, "Of course we knew something wasn't right. We kept asking, but you blew us off. We didn't know what to think — so we figured, maybe you're mad at us. We wanted to show our support and pride in our sister CSG. This party seemed like a kickin' idea. And look how many people showed —"

Miko interrupted, "You don't understand — this party is about everything I've been trying to get away from! Don't you guys get anything? You're supposed to be my friends!"

Dana, shaken now, put her arm around Miko's slim — if glittery — shoulders. "We are your friends. We never thought this would upset you. We only wanted to show you —"

"Show me what? What I already know? That I'm such a brainiac! That I always win at everything I try?" Miko practically spit the words out.

Softly, Nakili ventured, "Is that a bad thing?"

"Yes!" Miko, clearly frustrated, shouted.

Nakili prodded gently, "What's wrong with accomplishments? You're the shining example. . . ."

Miko, her lower lip trembling, croaked, "You don't get it! Everyone thinks of me as one-dimensional, like those . . . those . . . cardboard chess pieces you made! It's as if you purposely portrayed exactly what I don't want people to think about me!"

Rockett wished she could sink through the floor. "We didn't mean it like that," she whispered. It was the best she could offer.

Not trying to stop the tears now, Miko cried, "Don't you get it? Don't you see that I've been trying to change my image? I want people to look at me differently, as a cool person, not just 'Little Miss Can't Be Wrong.' I mean — Rockett, come *on*! You knew that! I even told you!"

Rockett swallowed hard but said nothing.

Miko shook her head. In a voice so quiet it was scary, she continued, "Sometimes I hate that things come so easily to me. Do people think I don't hear their comments? Like at the chess tournament. 'Oh, it's *her* again. Why bother even competing? She'll win. She always does.' The worst of it is, they're right."

Nakili tried, "But that's just some people. Not most people."

Miko turned to stare right into Nakili's eyes. "For once, I wanted to be popular, instead of envied. It's horrible to be resented."

To that, Nakili had no response.

Someone started to cry — and Rockett was shocked to realize it was Dana.

CHAPTER THIRTEEN

Rockett didn't know why, but she just knew: She *had* to say something. And it had to be better than good. It had to be so real, so meaningful, that it would turn this whole mess around. Precisely because she was outside of their circle, and not so emotionally involved, only she could get Miko back with her buds.

She took her best shot.

"Okay, so maybe I don't know you as well as they do. But in a way, maybe that's better. Maybe I see things more clearly. And here's how I see this, Miko. Please listen to me."

Miko peered at Rockett through mascara-tinted eyelashes. Her jaw was set, her arms folded. She stood ramrod straight.

And Rockett knew this wasn't going to be easy. She took a deep breath.

"Look, it doesn't matter what your image is. You have no better friends in the *world* than Nakili and Dana! You guys have a history. They know all parts of your personality — all the complications, layers. Mostly, they know your true heart."

Almost imperceptibly, Miko softened. But her arms still rested defensively in front of her chest.

Nakili's eyes were downcast. Dana had started to dab at her eyes.

Rockett continued, "As CSGs, you call yourselves sisters. Well, you are. Nakili and Dana were, like, the first ones to pick up on your gloomy vibes. And like Nakili said, they did try to find out what was wrong. When you didn't respond, did they go all, 'Whatever'? Did they drop you? No way!"

Dana stopped crying now. She listened intently to Rockett.

Nakili's head was still down.

Gathering steam now, Rockett went on. "They were so bummed that you seemed to be moving away from them. You never told them the real reason you were dressing and acting differently, so they assumed maybe it was because no one cheered when you won all that stuff. And then they were worried that maybe *you* thought the CSGs were breaking up. They never wanted that. Not for any reason."

And then the weirdest thing happened. At the exact same second, Dana choked up, Nakili looked up — and Miko teared up. Almost as if Rockett weren't there, an invisible magnet drew the three of them together, and the CSGs spontaneously embraced in a group hug. It was Dana who, seconds later, extended her arm to include Rockett.

Because they all had to do makeup repair, it took a while before four totally together and joyful friends emerged from the coat room. When they did, it was to the very distinct sound of an incredibly cool party in full swing. Arrow, Viva, and Ginger were rockin' the house, and everyone, it seemed, was up and dancing.

Jessie, who looked cute as a button in her sunflower-patterned jumper, was halfway around this twirl on the dance floor. She made eye contact with Miko and, flushed, trotted up. "Awesome party! We should do this more often. Even when it's not someone's birthday, or a holiday."

Miko agreed, "There's always something worth celebrating." Impulsively, she leaned forward and hugged Jessie. "I'm glad you're here."

Rockett tapped Jessie on the shoulder. "Me too, Jess."

Just then, Darnetta danced her way over and joined the little convo clutch. And then Mavis sauntered over. Sharla brought a soda for Miko, and Wolf came carrying a popcorn-filled paper bag. "Figured you might want some grub while there's still some left," he offered generously. "At these things, it's usually the guest of honor who never eats."

Miko grabbed a fistful of popcorn and happily stuffed her mouth, washing it down with a long, messy slurp of soda.

Before long, she was surrounded by her closest school friends. And it seemed to Rockett that the glow radiating from Miko had more to do with her innermost feelings than with any kind of makeup.

The only school friends who weren't encircling Miko at that moment were Nicole, Stephanie, and Whitney.

Instead, The Ones were tearing up the dance floor. Did they all just instinctively know the secret to looking cool when dancing? Rockett often felt she just looked all herky-jerky, uncoordinated. But her train of thought was interrupted by a sudden realization.

Where was Cleve? And Max? That had to be what Nicole was wondering. Every so often, and without missing a beat, Nicole looked around furtively, followed by a wristwatch-peeking time check.

So, I guess Cleve wasn't her date after all! Maybe I'll go up and point that out to Her Highness! But . . . how's Miko gonna feel when she realizes he's a no-show? Unless, of course, he's just being fashionably late. He and Max, that is.

Just then, someone tapped Rockett on the shoulder. She spun around, hoping for Miko's sake that it was Cleve.

"May I have the honor of this dance, m'lady?" Arnold Zeitbaum, all tuxed up and ready to rock 'n' roll . . . or something resembling that concept, anyway, was at Rockett's side.

She looked up at the hopeful, gawky boy. And smiled. "Sure, Arnie, I'd like that."

The song was "Jump High," the kind of catchy, rhythm's-gonna-get-you number that defies sitting out. And as Rockett bebopped with Arnold, she noted happily that the dance floor was filling up. It didn't surprise her that Nakili was shakin' her groove thing with Chaz, or that Dana had chosen Ruben to dance with. Nor was she really shocked to see Nicole lasso Wolf.

Okay, Jessie dancing with Bo Pezanski was a total head-scratcher . . . but more so was the boy Miko was with. Rockett sort of knew him. His name was Pete and he'd skipped a grade and so was in high school already.

She noted two things about him. Majorly drool-worthy was, okay, the first. But the other was the look on his face. He really seemed into Miko.

Rockett willed Cleve to show up right now. *Serves him right! How could he not be here? Even if he is seeing that other girl — this is Miko's night, he knows it!*

Her willing it, alas, did not make it so.

The song ended and still no Cleve, or Max, in sight. Everyone seemed to head over to the side of the room where the food had been set up. It was Dana's inspired idea to rent a popcorn and cotton candy wagon, which was stationed next to the snack and drink smorgasbord. Seeing the crowd filling up, Nakili noted, "I hope we got enough. This is one hungry bunch!"

Dana shrugged. "If we run out of food, we'll order some pizzas. Rockett's been so generous with her dough, I'm sure she'll spring for it!"

"Cute, Dana," Rockett said. Could she ever really be upset with her again, after what had happened tonight? At that moment, Rockett didn't think so.

Just then, the sound of someone tapping on the open mike muted all talk. Everyone turned to the stage. Arrow had come out from behind her drum set and addressed the crowd.

"Welcome to Miko's party!" she shouted, and everyone clapped. "Now that the festivities are in full swing, I'd like to announce a few happenin' events. Starting with this: I've convinced a very talented guitar player to join us for this next number. Believe me, it took a lot of convincing." She rolled her eyes to indicate "Not!"

That's when Ruben, guitar slung over his shoulder so casually, stepped up. Grinning into the crowd, he started to play a few chords. Arrow went back to her drum set, Viva and Ginger got ready, and Ruben led off, "One . . . two . . . three . . . four!" And just like that, they went into an incredibly cool swing dance number. Instantly, the party-goers were up and dancing.

Rockett was sweating when she stopped to get a drink. She surveyed the scene. The party, albeit bumpy at first, was going better than she could have imagined. She'd just gulped the last of her soda and was about to rejoin her dance buddies, when Miko came flying up to her. The hair clip was long gone, and the red-and-silver beaded thing was also missing in action. That alone made her seem more like the "old" Miko.

So did her floodlight smile. Tossing an arm around Rockett, she nodded at the stage. "I am so overwhelmed! It's totally taking me forever to realize how many people showed up! You guys did an unbelievable job."

Rockett shrugged. "They're all here for you, Miko." *Except Cleve.* She didn't say that out loud.

But Miko was on another train altogether. "What surprises me most is Ruben. Not only is he here, but he actually came up to me and gave me a peck on the cheek.

Which is Rubenese for 'The whole Herrera incident? I'm over it.'"

Rockett froze.

Miko cocked her head. "Are you all right?"

Hyperventilating, Rockett went, "Miko . . . there's something I need to tell you. Maybe this isn't the place, or the time, but . . . would you come with me for one second?"

The girls slipped out the nearest door. It led to the Olympic-sized pool. During the summer, it was always filled with the joyful splashing noises of neighborhood kids. Now the water was completely still.

In the moonlight, Miko's glitter sparkled. She teased, "So what's with the private, Rockett? Is this about Ruben? Are you two hooking up or something?"

For a split second, Rockett was stunned. "Why would you think that?"

"It's so obvious he likes you! These past few weeks, he was never mad at you for one second."

Rockett closed her eyes. "There's a reason for that. It has nothing to do with Ruben liking me. It's something I should have confessed a lot sooner, but . . . I couldn't."

Miko looked hyperconfused. "And now you can?"

"Tonight I realize how much your friendship means to me. I can't hold this in any longer. Because I told a lie. And that lie just, I don't know, puts a barrier between us." She took a deep breath. "Ruben wasn't mad at me because he didn't know the truth. And that's because I purposely lied to him."

"About what?"

"About turning him in to Principal Herrera. I told him *you* did it alone. That I was just sort of there, silent."

Miko's eyes widened. "Whoa, let me get this straight. Ruben thinks I went all tattletale to Herrera while you just, what, sat there and said nothing? Didn't agree or disagree?"

Rockett hung her head. "It's what he wanted to believe."

Now Miko wigged. "How could you do that?"

"Because . . ." Rockett struggled to find the right words. She knew there weren't any.

Suddenly, Miko shook her head. "I know! It's because he *expected* me to be the one — like I'm genetically incapable of not telling what I saw, right?"

At that instant, it hit Rockett like a speeding soccer ball, right to the gut: how frustrated it must make Miko feel to be labeled. "I'm really sorry. It stunk."

"You got that right — it did! And it does! That was totally lousy of you." Miko let Rockett have it — but at least she didn't stalk back into the party, angry. Instead, she began to pace back and forth, next to the pool, going, "I never expected you to be like this. I'm totally disappointed."

Rockett started to tear up. "And I'm totally ashamed, Miko."

Suddenly, Miko took a deep breath and seemed to make a snap decision. "I can't stay mad at you, Rockett. It's done, you told me the truth. We've all got our weak spots, maybe Ruben's just yours."

Relieved, Rockett earnestly said, "It won't happen again. I promise."

With a half smile, Miko allowed, "Anyway, I'm glad you finally told me. You didn't have to — I might never have found out. That took guts."

"So you forgive me?"

"Totally, let's go back inside. It's over."

"Not really, new girl. I guess in a way, it's just beginning!" The voice came from behind them. Rockett and Miko gasped in tandem and spun around. They'd never noticed that the music had stopped . . . and certainly never heard Ruben come outside. But there he was, arms folded, staring straight at them. Obviously, he'd heard enough of their exchange.

Rockett started to hyperventilate again. "I just didn't want you to hate me."

"Hate's a strong word, new girl, but I'm feeling pretty negative vibes right now. I don't know if I can deal with that." He turned and started to walk away.

Miko bolted after him and grabbed his elbow. "Wait, Ruben, I'm the one who should be mad. Not you."

"She lied to both of us," Ruben said, annoyed.

Maybe it was the edge to his voice — which hit Rockett as so unwarranted! *What's he got to be annoyed about?* Or maybe Rockett had just had enough. She got right in

Ruben's face. "I'm sorry you got in trouble, but you never should have put either of us on the spot like that! If you'd just copped to your bad, that would have been the end of it. You're great at making the music, Ruben — too bad you're not as good at facing it!"

They almost bumped into each other, trying to be the first to walk away. But Ruben had Rockett beat by a half-step.

Still outside, Miko turned to her. "I guess this wasn't destined to be a completely happy night."

"Actually, Miko, it was. And it is! I'm finally feeling clear about everything. If he can't see his way to what's right . . . what*ever*! Now, girlfriend — as Nakili would say — I hear a party going on inside, and I for one plan to be right in the middle of the fun. You coming?"

And for the next few hours, Rockett did exactly what she said. She danced her butt off. She laughed with her friends — *all* her friends. She not only participated in all the games, she *led* some of them.

Okay, so every once in a while, Rockett stole a glance at the door — to see if Cleve had turned up. It cheered her that Nicole seemed to be majorly wigged, which if Miko noticed, didn't let it bum her out.

If only Cleve had stayed away.

CHAPTER FOURTEEN

When Cleve did show up, he was accompanied by Max. And a major melee. Was the boy merely incapable of slipping into a party in progress unobtrusively? Or was his noisy entrance, and everything that followed, Nicole's fault?

It went down like this. Rockett was at the head of the conga line. She wasn't sure what possessed her to lead the twenty-five dancers, attached to one another by hands on waists, outside the rec room, but half the party was dancing around the periphery of the pool when the noise level abruptly amped up.

It was Nicole who broke from the wiggly line first, that was for sure. Over the music, she shouted, "Cleve! You're here! Come dance with me!" She didn't give him a chance to decide if he wanted to, but flew up to him and grabbed his arm. Nicole was all about making sure everyone at the party "got" that they were a couple.

Not that Cleve fought it. Sheepishly, he allowed her to act possessive. Theatrically, she smooched him on the cheek, then slipped her arm around his waist and pulled him to her.

Nicole was an excellent show-off. Good enough to

stop the conga line. Good enough to start Rockett on a slow burn.

More significantly, it was good enough to tick Nakili off. She marched up and pointed a sharp finger at Cleve's chin. "Best mind your manners, Cleve! Showin' up late stinks, but not even giving a shout-out to the guest of honor? Do I have to remind you, she's a very special friend of yours?"

Miko ran over and got on diffuse-patrol. "It's fine if Cleve wants to dance with Nicole first. He'll get around to saying hey to me, right, Cleve?"

No one really got that Miko was sincere. No one got it fast enough, anyway.

Certainly, Nicole didn't. She just gave new depth and scope to the term *territorial*. "Cleve is here as my date."

"Your date who came late," Dana, who never shied from a chance at one-ups, tossed in. That might have really started the hubbub.

But it was Sharla who seconded that commotion. "Your date who came so late, maybe *you* don't really rate!"

"Whoo-hoo! Good one, Norvell!" Dana slapped her five, egging her on. Which brought Nicole's loyal troops into the about-to-be free-for-all.

"What's the difference when he got here?" Stephanie demanded. "The boy is here, and he's with who he chooses to be with. That, as anyone can see, is Nicole. Not Miko."

Rockett's slow burn began to gather speed. She took a step in Cleve's direction, when abruptly he detached himself from Nicole and casually, as if no one had reprimanded him, sauntered close to Miko.

"Hey, you," he said with a grin. Then he touched Miko's chin to tilt her face up to his. "Guest-of-honor-girl. Congratulations, Meeks. You deserve this party — you look amazing. And everyone knows how cool you are."

Was Cleve really about to kiss Miko, in front of everyone?

As if Nicole would ever let anyone find out! Because humiliation was not on her personal agenda, she erupted in a spontaneous hissy fit. "And you, Cleve, deserve an Academy Award! Everyone knows how cool she isn't! Little Miss Brainiac is so style-devoid and personality-challenged, she couldn't catch a boyfriend if he were the common cold!"

"Look who's talking!" Rockett exploded. Charging up to Nicole, she spewed, "Like you know anything! I have a little bombshell for you!"

If Rockett had thought about it, she might have tried to spare Miko's feelings. But at that moment, she was beyond furious at Nicole, and that went double for Cleve. How dare he be such a two-timing, insincere sleaze!

So she just blurted it all out.

"I can tell you why Cleve was late tonight. And why he's been out of afternoon classes so often. Cleve has a girlfriend! Her name is Cindy and she goes to high school, so he ducks out early to see her!"

Rockett ignored the gasps of disbelief. Once she'd blasted off, her allegations zoomed through the night air, spinning uncontrollably. "And there's more . . . ! How does he get permission to leave school early? He doesn't! And at Whistling Pines, we have a name for that — cutting! And that's why Mrs. Herrera is all over him!"

Whether Nicole ever heard the second part of Rockett's verbal grenade was debatable. And probably inconsequential. All she had to hear was the name Cindy. She lost it.

"How dare you!" she screamed. With a fury propelled by deep embarrassment, she charged at him. Tragically for Cleve, his back was to the swimming pool. Worse, he'd been standing only a few inches from the edge.

The *ka-boom* splash he made going in was almost louder than his shouts of stunned horror. But Cleve rebounded quickly. A strong swimmer, he was at the side of the pool in no time — close enough to grasp Nicole by her ankle. She never had a chance. In a nanosecond, he'd dragged her in!

Rockett would have thought the other Ones — Stephanie and Whitney — might have retaliated on behalf of their drenched leader. But on second thought, what happened next could have been scripted. It was Dana and Sharla who grooved on the splash scene. Without real cause, except that he was Cleve's ally, tall

Dana dived after diminutive Max, sending him flying over the edge, while Sharla dragged poor, unsuspecting Chaz in! "He goes with the two of them" was her "logic takes a holiday" reasoning.

Nakili sprung into action. She ran inside, intending to grab the cordless mike and take charge. But her screams of "Stop the insanity!" brought the adults running outside. Miko's parents, with strong support from Nakili's and Dana's, were the ones who finally helped drag the kids out of the pool.

They also declared this party officially over.

Hours later, only the cleanup committee remained. Aside from Rockett and the CSGs, the other volunteers were Jessie, Arrow, Ginger, Viva, Wolf, and sorta surprisingly, Ruben, who explained, "Hey, my curfew's not till midnight, and this boy's been on lockdown long enough to want to make the most of another hour of freedom. Even if it does mean bagging the garbage."

"I'm with you, dude," Wolf offered, and started clearing what was left of the food. Arrow and her band began breaking down the stage.

Meanwhile, Miko, Rockett, Nakili, Dana, and Jessie ambled over to the back of the room and started tearing down the crepe paper and other decorations. The girls worked in silence for a while, until Miko broke it.

"I knew, you know."

Her friends stopped what they were doing. "You knew what?" Nakili asked.

"I knew about Cleve. And about Cindy. And even about the whole cutting thing."

Stunned silence greeted her admission.

Finally, Dana said, "If you knew he was seeing this Cindy person, how could you continue to go out with him?"

Miko closed her eyes and shook her head. Then, she plopped down in the middle of the floor and held her head in her hands. Rockett, Nakili, Dana, and Jessie didn't need to be told to join her. In a second, they'd formed a little circle on the floor. Where Miko explained everything.

"Cleve and I were never boyfriend and girlfriend. I mean — hello! I was trying a new image, I didn't have a personality transplant!"

No one laughed. "Two big questions, Miko," Dana said. "Why'd you let everyone think you were? And what accounts for spending so much time together? Don't deny it. We saw you two in the mall, looking awfully cozy."

Miko sighed. "I never really knew Cleve all that well. I mean, until Mrs. Herrera threw us together so I could tutor him, I just thought he was nothing more than a superficial jock, a real flirt. And what's funny is that he thought I was just a boring little brainiac. I think maybe we were both out to prove the other one wrong."

"You mean, Cleve's more than a superficial jock?" Dana asked. "I don't think so."

"He really is. He's got layers, like all of us. Like you, Dana — and like me."

Dana wasn't buying it. "Need proof."

Miko sighed. "He's got all these family complications. It's not my place to tell about Cleve's private life, but let's just say it was easy for him to pretend his real father blew into town and signed the 'excused absence' forms. He knew Mrs. Herrera would have trouble contacting his dad. And it's not like he even gets along with his stepdad."

"That still doesn't explain why you let everyone think you were a twosome," Jessie, whose own parents were divorced, pointed out.

To that Miko shrugged. "I don't know, I just wanted to see what it felt like to have people saying something about me that didn't have to do with what award I just got, or what test I just aced, or how I'm genetically incapable of fibbing."

Rockett tilted her head. "How did it feel?"

Miko paused. "Good at first. But it got out of hand. Nicole went off on me, and that hurt. I wasn't all that secure with trying a different style. I guess the worst was when I thought you guys didn't like me anymore."

"Hello, we were planning your party!" Dana, exasperated, yelled.

"Well, I know that now! But then, it seemed like just because I was trying a different look and spending time with Cleve, you were abandoning me or something."

Just then, Arrow hit the drums, and the girls all twisted around to see what she was doing. "I just remembered," Arrow told them. "We never got to perform that song we wrote."

"You wrote a song?" Miko asked.

"We did. Remember when I was saying we had a lot of special surprises tonight? Well, we didn't get to all of them. Most people went home, but . . . what do you say, Jessie? You up for it?"

Rockett was confused. "Jessie?"

Getting up, Jessie grinned. "I was going to sing with Arrow's band tonight. That's why I couldn't help with the decorating. I was rehearsing with them."

Rockett grinned. "Go for it, Jess!"

With that, Arrow and the Explorers — unplugged now, since they'd almost finished cleaning up — started to play. And Jessie sang. The song was called "Miko." It was about the unbreakable bonds of friendship.

Listening to the words, Rockett teared up. She almost didn't notice the boy who'd quietly come to stand next to her. Until, that is, he took her hand.

"Dance with me, new girl?"

Rockett caught her breath, turned, and looked into Ruben's deep brown eyes. "So you're not mad at me anymore?"

"That's the question I should be asking you. Forgive me, *chica*? For everything?"

"I just want us to be friends, Ruben. Friends who don't put each other on the spot. Friends who tell each other the truth."

"You got it, Rockett."

The song, and the dance, had just ended when Dana started to jump up and down. "I can't believe it! We forgot to give Miko her gift!"

"It's not too late." Nakili dashed over to the side of the room where it had been propped up, wrapped and tied with a huge bow.

"Hey, you guys," Miko said, "I don't need a gift. This party said it all. I know who my friends are. And I know who I am. Besides, these platform shoes are killing my feet and I think I'm allergic to glitter — it's giving me a rash! If it's okay with you guys, I think I might . . . uh . . . rewind the image tape. 'Cause I think maybe the people who *count* like me just the way I am."

Dana rolled her eyes. "Mushiness-alert! Open it already!"

Miko burst into such hysterics when she did, her parents came flying over to make sure she was all right. "This is the most amazing thing anyone's ever done for me," she managed through her sobs. "I . . . I . . ."

"A simple thank-you will do!" Dana laughed, and hugged her bud.

"And," Miko's mom interjected, "a few more hands will simply do so we can finish this cleanup!"

As Rockett helped separate the recyclables from the rest of the mess, she thought about the spontaneous group hug that had occurred in the coat room at the beginning of the party. And suddenly, she had a major bolt of inspiration. "Hey, Miko, can I have the gift for a sec?"

Miko feigned suspicion. "You're not taking it back, are you?"

"I'm adding something to it."

And so the collage Miko went home with that night had this postscript: "The coolest discovery true friends can make is that they can grow separately without growing apart."

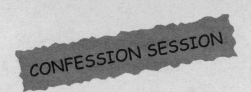

ABOUT THE AUTHOR

Lauren Day: Pseudonym-alert! My real name is Randi Reisfeld and I've written lots of books for teens and 'tweens. Maybe you've read some. I've done a bunch in the *Clueless* series (based on the classic movie and TV show); the *Moesha* series; *Meet the Stars of Animorphs*; and *Prince William: The Boy Who Will Be King*, to cite a few that are circa now. Then there's *Got Issues Much? Celebrities Share Their Traumas and Triumphs*, where today's top young stars tell how they got through the tough times. Landing in *Rockett's World* is my coolest writing gig so far — I hope you come along for all the journeys.

Rockett's World ™

GET READY!
GET SET!
READ ROCKETT!

$3.99 each

Meet me at Purple Moon®

www.purple-moon.com

Find out more about these great CD-ROM titles!

Rockett's CAMP Adventures™
CD-ROM

Camp brings new friends and experiences ... are you ready?

SECRET PATHS To Your Dreams™
CD-ROM

What do dreams mean?

MATTEL MEDIA™